Praise for Gayle Hanratty's

GRAY HAMPTON: A SUITE OF STORIES

Because these short stories comprise a "suite," they should be read in order, just as, say, the parts of a Bach *Suite for Unaccompanied Cello* should be heard serially. There's huge variety among these stories and significant silences between them. Gayle Hanratty's use of form recreates the very way we both experience and remember our lives. Defined moments, snatched from the flow of time, create vibrant and significant meaning. While Hanratty's suite of stories has caught time on the wing, each moment and each individual story digs its toes into the real earth. These stories have the toughness and truth-telling of authentic tenderness extended toward our human condition.

Sena Jeter Naslund

editor, Fleur-de-Lis Press, & author of *Ahab's Wife*, *Four Spirits*, *The Fountain of St. James Court, or Portrait of the Artist as an Old Woman*, & six others

This lovely book is a meditation on everyday people whose lives are normal yet magical, quiet yet never dull. Gayle Hanratty has fashioned a complex, living world and a memorable cast of characters with a precise and wise understanding of the human heart.

Silas House

author of *The Coal Tattoo* & *A Parchment of Leaves*

The characters in Gayle Hanratty's Gray Hampton are bursting with life, as indelible as the setting that shapes them. Deftly (and boldly) spanning almost a century, as well as multiple points of view, through several generations of a single family, this glorious suite of stories is imbued with the author's clear eye and good heart.

Robin Lippincott

author of *Blue Territory: A Meditation on the Life and Art of Joan Mitchell*, and *Rufus + Syd*

Gray Hampton is a deeply felt, at times darkly humorous collection, brimming with complicated, vivid characters, as tough and tenacious as briars. Gayle Hanratty has peopled her book with characters who are not only brave, self-reliant and unforgettable; they are also tender in fleeting, startling, and profoundly affecting ways. These stories will break your heart and will remind you of the things that matter most in this life.

Eleanor Morse

author of *White Dog Fell from the Sky*

GRAY HAMPTON

GRAY HAMPTON

A Suite of Stories

by

GAYLE HANRATTY

Fleur-de-Lis Press 2017
Louisville, Kentucky

This is a work of fiction. Names, characters, and incidents are products
of the author's imagination or are used fictitiously. Any resemblance
to actual events or persons, living or dead, is entirely coincidental.

Cover by Monica Mahoney & Jonathan Weinert
Book design by Jonathan Weinert

Printed in the United States of America
First Edition

Library of Congress Cataloging-in-Publication Data
Hanratty, Gayle
Gray Hampton.
I. Title
Library of Congress Control Number: 2017939796

ISBN 10: 0-9960120-1-X
ISBN 13: 978-0-9960120-1-0

Fleur-de-Lis Press of *The Louisville Review*
Spalding University
851 S. Fourth Street
Louisville, KY 40203
502.873.4398
louisvillereview@spalding.edu
www.louisvillereview.org

CONTENTS

GRAY HAMPTON

People called us trash—all us Skinners.

Daddy was a sharecropper when he wasn't drunk. The man didn't own so much as a cow. My brothers fought and drank too, and one of my sisters was well known for her wanton ways. Even the milkweed and briars that skirted our borrowed house keeled over in disgrace.

If only I had been as lucky as those weeds, as dying seemed easier than living as a Skinner. It would take years and too many mistakes for me to learn that we weren't all trash.

The worst disgrace happened the morning I was hurrying to school with everybody else who lived on our side of town. To keep from being late, we had to leave home in time to get past the tracks before the 8:12 roared through. It was the longest train of the day and had been the cause of many an unjust tardy slip.

A boy named G.W. Shumate was in our group. I'd had an awful crush on him all through ninth grade, though he didn't know it. I held to the back of the crowd so G.W. wouldn't notice my shabby coat and shoes. Even though he was poor too, G.W. was well thought of, and he had a way of making a tattered wool sweater and scarred leather cap look smart. I possessed no such grace.

When we got near the tracks, somebody yelled, "Look here!"

It wasn't until I got closer that I saw my own Daddy lying there with one of his legs splayed across the rail. Everybody started to laugh; some even kicked at him.

"Let's take his money," one kid said.

"Looks like Moony Flynn's done got it all." G.W. was talking about the local moonshine runner.

I could've died then and there, and was wishing for that very thing when every head in the bunch jerked as the 8:12's whistle began to squall. It was January and cold and the steam from the locomotive left a sideways trail as it lumbered around the curve. I never even flinched—thinking Daddy was about to get exactly what he deserved. It sounded far off and lonesome and I imagined someday it would carry me out of this hell called Gray Hampton. Watching the 8:12 approach, I thought how that late train's whistle would soon serve a very different reminder.

I wanted to see it happen; to watch Jake Skinner, no-good father, husband, son, and brother, get his just desserts. But then G.W. and some of the others grabbed hold of Daddy's legs and dragged him to the shoulder.

"Shoo wee," he said, screwing up his face as he let Daddy's limp ankles flop against the gravel.

"Did he pee himself?" somebody asked, pointing to the dark

shadow spread across the groin of the old man's trousers.

"Smells like he done worse than that," G.W. said as the train rumbled past us. Our eyes met for an instant as he strutted in my direction. The way he had his hand up to his mouth, I thought he might be about to whisper something comforting to me, or kindly touch my shoulder. Instead, as G.W. marched past me, he spit right on the toes of my shoes and then he crowed, "Or maybe that's just Skinner perfume."

Fourteen years old, I quit school at that exact minute, too ashamed to go back, and too mortified to ever see G.W. Shumate again. I figured it didn't much matter—educated or not—nobody in Gray Hampton would ever want a Skinner for a girlfriend.

I'd known Ivan Barkley my whole life when he showed up at the barn that day in '36. He claimed he was looking for my brothers. A couple of my girl cousins and me were fixing to ride the farmer's horses. They'd strapped saddles on theirs, but I didn't need anything between me and my sweaty colt. I always rode Demon. That horse and me shared a starving need—to run as fast and as far as his legs and my behind could last.

"Jump on," I called, patting Demon's rump. "Russell and Anthony are off somewhere with Daddy." I heard one of my cousins suck in air and the other say, "Saalll," making my name sound like it had two syllables.

Maybe it was the way the sun lit a fire around him when he

strolled out of the bright daylight into the dim barn, or maybe it was because I was so desperate to get away. But I decided then and there that Ivan Barkley would be the one to take me away from Gray Hampton, and Daddy, and the rest of my clan.

Ivan hopped on Demon's back and loosed his arms around my waist. I leaned forward like I was telling Demon my secret, shook the reins, and dug my heels into the horse's flanks. He reared up and charged off like the one he was named for. I felt Ivan tighten his hold as we flew under limbs and over fences and right through the middle of puddles. When we slowed up at the creek, Ivan jumped off like his butt was on fire. His hair was blown back, mud was splattered all over his face, and his legs were wobbly as a new foal's. He staggered backwards and sputtered, "My God, girl, are you possessed or something?"

"I'm just trying to get somewhere fast," I said, dropping down to the ground. "Wet your hands here in the creek. Your face looks like you've been rooting slop." He bent down and politely obeyed my direction. I untied the bandana from around my neck and offered it to him to dry off.

Shivers coiled from my tailbone clear out my ears when he laid his hands on either side of my waist to boost me back atop Demon. I took it easier on the ride back to enjoy the feel of him behind me.

Nobody called a Barkley trash. Ivan's papa, Mr. Jim, owned a trucking business that made him about the most prosperous man in Gray

Hampton. The Mayor himself counted Mr. Jim among his personal advisors. But it wasn't only Ivan's name and family standing that I was after, he had good manners, he was handsome, and a good dresser too—always wore a brown felt hat and matching wool coat when we went out. Even though he wasn't too tall, he was well built and looked strong. And his eyes—his eyes were the color of Virginia bluebells in late April.

When we'd go dancing, he'd act like I was the only girl in the room. He preferred the slow dances to the jitterbugs and I did too—just for the chance to hold each other close and to breathe his clean smell. For the life of me, I couldn't figure why such a fine man cared a whit about me, a Skinner. Ivan said we were just like "oil and water" as the saying goes, "we go together a lot better once we shake things up." And he was right about that.

On January 27, 1938, we got married. Then, when the army took him to Alaska for what seemed liked forever, I thought maybe I'd made a mistake and that I'd never get out of this town. But by 1940, Mr. and Mrs. Ivan Barkley had moved into a house in Louisville—bought and paid for with Barkley money.

I'd finally done it—gotten out of Gray Hampton, out of Skinner hell. In Louisville, nobody would know how my Daddy had passed out on the tracks, or how I'd had to wear ragged clothes. No one here would ever spit on me or tell me I smelled bad. I would never be called trash again—thanks to Ivan Barkley.

Before marrying Ivan I didn't know men could be so kind. I figured they all got mean drunk and then used it as an excuse to beat on their wives and kids. Unlike the men I was accustomed to, Ivan loved children—our nieces and nephews, as well as our own two girls. Nicole and Penny were only thirteen months apart. Nicole was born first. She had dark hair and skin, like me. Her hair curled around her face like a china doll. Penny was fair and as white-headed as cotton. She favored Ivan and became Mr. Jim's darling the minute he glimpsed her Barkley blue eyes.

About a year after Penny came along, in late 1944, Ivan started working for Wittenberg Construction—and that's when all the trouble started. The crew had a habit of stopping off for beers after work at a place called Ott's Tavern. Ivan joined right in with them like it'd been his custom all along. For a long time, it was just on Fridays, then on Wednesdays too. It was starting to seem to me like Ivan would sooner go out drinking with his buddies than be at home—just like my Daddy. Ivan was kicking me right back to Gray Hampton. Just the thought of him out drinking at a tavern made me feel like I smelled bad, like trash. I couldn't stand it if people thought of my girls that way.

"Mama, is there any happy cake left?" Penny asked. It was Wednesday evening and we'd just celebrated her fourth birthday the night before. The girls and I'd already eaten supper and Ivan still wasn't home.

"I'll cut you some as soon as you both finish your peas."

Then right when I was slicing the cake for the girls, in he saunters like everything was hunky-dory. I grabbed a hunk of icing and threw it at him. He ducked and the gooey mess smooshed against one of the white metal kitchen cabinets. The girls laughed hard not knowing how mad I was, but Ivan knew. He gave everything away with his eyes. The way they jumped back and forth I could tell he was trying to figure out a way to keep the peace. Finally he said, "Why don't you girls take your cake out to the picnic table."

They were no sooner out the door when I said, "I won't have a husband that can't stand to come home." Then I took a swing at him. He ducked again, but I grazed his lip with my ring.

He wiped his lip on the back of his hand and looked down to see if there was blood. There was, but not much. He drew his bottom lip into his mouth and sucked on it a minute while his eyes burned into me. Instead of the hateful glare I'd expected from such wildness, I saw only love in his eyes. He picked up a paper napkin to dab at his lip, speaking between the dabs—finally breaking the impossible silence that had overtaken my kitchen.

"All I'm doing is unwinding with the crew after a hard day. It doesn't have anything to do with you, Sal." He licked blood off his lip. "There's nothing I enjoy more than being at home with you and the girls."

Despite his words, I knew what he had to be thinking; I'd heard Daddy say it to my mother over and over: *You're the one drives me to drink—always nagging me about something. No wonder I can't stand to come home.*

"I'd sooner be alone than with a man won't come home nights.

You might as well move out of here." I knew his only choice was to move in with his mama and papa in Gray Hampton. "We'll see what your papa thinks about that."

"The guys make fun of me if I don't stop off a night or two with them, Billy goes too. It's kind of expected," Ivan said, trying to convince me.

But neither his reasoning nor the spilling of his blood satisfied me. The only thing he could have said that would have made it right was: "I won't be going out with the fellas anymore." Knowing those words weren't coming, I crossed my arms to emphasize how determined I was.

Seeing that I was set on it, he said, "If you won't let me stay, at least let me take one of the girls with me."

I had my mouth set to say *no* when another idea tiptoed into my mind. I wanted his papa, Mr. Jim, to think I was trying to be fair. So I said, "You can take Penny with you." My hope was that if it looked like I was being reasonable, Mr. Jim would soon show Ivan the error of his ways.

Ivan's shoulders shuddered and his eyes squinted. I wondered if he saw that I was conniving in letting him take Penny with him; that I was using our own daughter for a bargaining chip. I actually surprised myself at the lengths I'd go to get my way.

As quickly as I'd said he could take her, homesickness balled up in my throat. It was a lump that would stay there the entire time Penny was gone. But, I was not going to live with a man who acted like my Daddy. The only difference between Ivan and Jake Skinner was that I knew Ivan would be good to Penny. There was no doubt about that.

"I guess it's settled then. We'll leave Friday night." He checked on Nicole and Penny through the screen door.

After our split his sister Rita told me that some evenings Ivan was too tired to make the drive back to Gray Hampton, so he'd sleep on her couch. Her husband, Billy, worked the same job as Ivan for Wittenberg. They were building grain silos at Ballard Flour Mills—a job they were about to finish. Wittenberg always had more work for them—good carpenters were hard to find.

People told me I ought to be glad Ivan had such a good job, instead of the places a lot of men had to work—like the Falls City Brewery or Brown and Williamson. Those places worked their men half to death—making them put in extra hours without paying overtime. Then they tried to buy them off by giving every man a case of beer or a carton of cigarettes every Friday at quitting time. Working for Wittenberg might have been more dangerous than those other places, but they were fair and square with the men's time and money.

With Ivan and Penny gone, the house was hauntingly quiet. Cooking was hardly worth the effort for just Nicole and me. So I usually fixed us cold cereal or eggs or pancakes. But it was the nights that swallowed me up and there was that nagging lump in my throat for Penny. Nicole had trouble getting to sleep without Penny there, too. She'd cry and cry and ask, "Where's my Penny, when's Poppy coming home?" It about killed me to see her so sad and lonesome.

Billy and Rita invited Nicole and me to their house for supper one night. I brought macaroni and cheese and they fixed an oven chicken and green beans. It was the best meal we'd eaten all week. I asked how Ivan was doing and Billy said that Ivan said he wanted to come home, but that I wouldn't let him. I said I'd let him if he'd quit going to Ott's.

I was miserable without him. I craved the heat of him in my bed and the soothe of his snoring on the back of my neck. Plus, if I didn't lay eyes on Penny soon, my throat was going to close up all the way. So after just two Saturdays, I gulped hard and asked Rita and Billy to drive us to Gray Hampton.

When we got there, Nicole ran to find her sister. She knew where she'd be—playing dolls with her cousins. Billy and Rita followed after her with their brood. I wanted to follow them—to see Penny, but first things first.

In just the short walk from Billy's car to the house, I could feel every eye in Gray Hampton studying me—wondering why Ivan Barkley had ever married Salinda Skinner. I could still picture how that Clara Pike had elbowed her sister and whispered to her at our wedding. I was walking up the aisle of the church when I had heard her declare: "What would Ivan want with a stick like her; bosoms the size of chicken eggs." Then her sister snickered back, "Yeah, fried." The whole town whispered it: No such thing as a pretty Skinner even if you are good looking.

I talked to myself all the way up the sidewalk trying to put their ridicule out of my head. "You're not a Skinner anymore, your name is Sal Barkley." Before I knocked, I smoothed the seams of my hose and brushed at the lap wrinkles in my dress—all to keep from inspecting my shoes for spit. It wasn't an easy habit to break.

I knocked on the screen door. Ivan seemed surprised to see me. "Don't you look fine in your yellow dress. You look as pretty as a bunch of daffodils." He gave me a quick kiss, grinned, and walked me toward the back of the house where he and his papa had been passing the time in the kitchen. Mr. Jim stood with his back to the sink—arms folded across his rich-man's belly. Ivan and me sat next to each other on the far side of the table. It felt right to be sitting next to him again.

Mr. Jim was taller than his son and he had those same blue eyes, only his lacked the tender look of Ivan's. Even though he was past seventy, Mr. Jim cut a powerful figure. As he glided around the kitchen, a reminder of him seemed to linger in the previous spot.

"What brings you to town, Sal, running low on money?" Mr. Jim asked as he set two clean glasses on the green speckled counter.

I ignored his insult, sucked in a big swig of air, and started to explain why I had come. I wanted him to hear my reasons why Ivan and me had separated. "I don't know if Ivan's told you much about our problems. But it's mainly because of how he stops off at Ott's Tavern two times a week with that bunch from work—Billy goes too. From what I'm used to, it can only get worse."

This whole time Mr. Jim was making highballs. He opened a high cabinet and set the whiskey back inside. Then he filled the glasses to the brim with a light colored mixer. I wondered why he'd be fixing drinks now—not even three o'clock in the afternoon. Was he making fun of me?

My eyes followed him while I continued to spell it out, "They leave their wives sitting at home wearing frumpy old house dresses and can't even buy shoes for their babies. If Ivan keeps this up, I won't have any choice but to file for a divorce." As soon as I'd said it, a vague chill settled over the room like somebody had opened a door somewhere and Mr. Jim dropped his spoon in the sink, letting it make a startling clatter.

I glimpsed Ivan's distressing stare. This was the first he'd heard me make any mention of a divorce and I knew he was as shocked as Mr. Jim.

When Ivan and me got married, I converted from nothing to a Catholic, the Barkley's religion. I knew Catholics were against divorce. So I thought by saying that I would file, it would get Mr. Jim to tell Ivan to shape up.

I wasn't even close to finished when Mr. Jim butted in. "Ivan and Bill work hard, Sal," he said as he dipped a swizzle stick into the liquid. "There's nothing wrong with them having a drink some nights with their pals." He wiped off the bottom of each glass with a towel. "Besides, these men have got more serious things to talk about than dresses and baby shoes. It's not like he's running around. He and the boys are just blowing off a little steam." He folded the cloth and hung it back on the towel bar.

I was starting to feel a bit steamed myself. Ivan must have sensed it too because he'd started to fidget in his chair, rubbing his knee with his palm. I truly did not understand how Mr. Jim could possibly defend Ivan's behavior. I knew for a fact that Mr. Jim did his drinking at home.

Mr. Jim walked to the end of the table to hand Ivan his highball. When he reached the tumbler past me, I shot out of my chair and halted his serving hand. Standing eyeball to eyeball with the most respected man in Gray Hampton, I spewed a ball of spit directly into that perfectly mixed and swizzled concoction. Maybe a little bit hit his hand too. Then I plopped down and held my head high—proud I'd done it. My Skinner green eyes blazed into Mr. Jim Barkley's baby blues.

Mr. Jim towered at the end of the table like a judge in a court of law. I saw him raise his arm up past his shoulder and I stiffened for the sound of his hand smacking the table like a gavel. Instead, the man known for his tolerance and charity hauled off and slapped me right across the face. Ivan jumped half a foot, like he'd been the one hit.

"Papa!" Ivan hollered. And I heard myself let out a tiny "uhh," even though I tried to sit quiet and not give him the satisfaction of knowing how bad he'd hurt me. But with the sting of it and the shock, a little air must have seeped out.

He could've been God standing there—judging what to do next. Nobody talked. It was like we were measuring each other's breathing. I looked at Ivan and saw a tear roll down his cheek. I felt his hand on my leg and wondered when he'd put it there. My spine wanted to bend and curl in shame, but I forced myself to sit up straight. I wondered how Ivan could just sit there hunkered over and let his papa treat me worse than a dog—like a Skinner.

Finally, Mr. Jim spoke. And this time, he let us both have it.

"Catholics do not and you will not get divorced! I'll see you dead before I'll let that happen." His voice boomed like a preacher's as he paced the pine floor and gestured with his arms. "And wives ought to do right by their husbands. I'll not have some yellow-dressed hellion storm into my house threatening a divorce, when it seems to me like you ought to be glad you got a man comes from a good family, not some drunken bastard like your daddy and the rest of the Skinners."

The table moaned as he leaned in to get a close fix on Ivan and me. He shook a finger in our faces and said, "I hear any more talk about a divorce and I guarantee you'll both have hell to pay." He walked away, then turned and added, "I'll leave the two of you to chew on just exactly how it is that hell gets paid." Then, he was out the door.

I wanted to vomit.

Ivan moved his grip from my knee to my hand. "Sal, let's go home. I'll try harder." He wet a towel in the sink, then pressed its warmth against the red blotch left on my cheek by Mr. Jim's mitt of a hand. I felt more gentleness in the blue-eyed son's touch than his papa possessed in a lifetime. I wanted to think that Ivan could try harder, but I knew better. Even if he promised he would stay away from Ott's, I knew saying "no" when he was face-to-face with his heckling buddies was more than he would be able to bear. It's how he was, wanting to please everybody.

"Where's Nicole and Penny?" I asked, dislodging his hand and the cloth from my jaw. "Neither of them was in here were they?" I asked in fear they might have seen me be humiliated.

"They're still off playing." Ivan put his hand under my elbow to lift me out of the chair and repeated, "Let's go home, we'll be all right." Letting Ivan guide me, I knew I'd lost. This whole separation had gained me nothing and only worsened my favor with Mr. Jim. Still, I let Ivan steer me.

Feeling dazed, I gathered up the girls and scooted them into the backseat of the car. Ivan held the front door open for me. He held my hand as I folded onto the flannel seat. He tucked the hem of my yellow dress inside and gently pushed the door shut. He opened the trunk and filled it with all the things he and Penny had brought.

The trip home was quiet, and I shivered more than once at the memory of Mr. Jim's slap and his threat that there'd "be hell to pay." The smoke from our cigarettes mingled with the shame and the guilt and flooded the Ford with a foggy, unnatural peace.

"How about we stop up here at the A&W for root beers?" I ignored the fake excitement in Ivan's voice. "You want one, Sal?" I shook my head. He ordered four drinks anyway.

"Poppy, I want a hot dog," Nicole said.

"Not me," Penny said.

The girls played in the back seat—Penny with her dolls, and Nicole coloring in her book, while they quietly downed their drinks and hot dog. They'd already learned to keep still during times like these. Later when we passed the twin spires of the horse track, Nicole failed to toot the "Call to The Post" and Penny didn't bother singing "the sun shines bright," the way they usually did.

Derby week soon rolled round. Ivan had bought us a radio so we could listen to the horse races and broadcasts of Pee Wee Reese's ballgames. After the Dodgers played, I turned the dial to WHAS and listened to them interview the Andrews Sisters who'd come to town to see the seventy-fifth Run for the Roses.

Everybody in Louisville celebrated some during Derby week. So on Wednesday afternoon, I scooped Nicole and Penny up in my arms and whispered, "How about we play dress-up?" I let them pick out what they wanted to wear. They pulled out their Easter dresses and I put on my good dress too and smeared on some lipstick, a color called Coral-bells. I even found a yellow scarf to match my dress and tied it around my hair like I'd seen Maxine Andrews do in the *Screen Romances* magazine. We thought it would be great fun to surprise their poppy in all our finery.

"Mama, Gina wants lipstick too," Nicole said, holding up her doll. We must have spent over two hours primping and preening.

The girls didn't seem to mind, or even notice when Ivan was late, but I felt such rage building, I thought I'd burst. It was the first time he'd stayed out since we'd gotten back together. At their bedtime, I was rough-handed putting Penny's pajamas on her, jerking her little arms through the sleeves harder than I needed to. Nicole's brow was crinkled with a worried frown and she got into her PJs by herself.

Why weren't they as disappointed as I was, I wondered? Wasn't the fun in seeing how he'd act when he saw the three of us wearing our Derby outfits? I kept it inside just long enough to kiss the girls goodnight.

I studied my reflection in the hall mirror. The twig of a woman imaged there with full lips and deep-set green eyes stared back at me. Ivan once told me there were times when he thought my eyes looked as ferocious as a wild cat's. I could see that very thing now, mocking me in the mirror. "He'd come straight home if you weren't so ugly," I told the image.

The scarf I'd tied around my hair looked silly now. I yanked it off and tore toward the kitchen. I hiked myself up on the table and sat cross-legged smack in the middle of it with that yellow dress stretched across my knees, and I waited fifteen minutes, then thirty, and at about eight I heard the front door creak.

Inside me something said: *If Daddy's drunk, he'll beat the first one he sees.*

"Quick, hide!" I heard myself say out loud. That's the way it would have been when I was little, but not now.

"Hidy Sal," Ivan beamed. "What're you doing all dressed up in the middle of the kitchen table on a Wednesday night?" He hung his hat on the coat rack and flashed me his best Bogart grin.

I leaped off the table panting and clawing so hard that I split my dress up the side. "Supper ruined while you were out drinking," I snarled. "You're the one acting like trash now." I sprayed words and threats like I had a mouthful of tacks.

"Jesus, Sal, I'm sorry about supper, but you don't have to go wild over it." He headed toward the sink. "I told you this morning I'd be late, that we were all going to Ott's." His face was as pained as I'd seen it with furrows plowed deep between his eyes. "Look what you done to your dress."

"What I've done? You're the one who's done it." And when I swung around to hit him, he grabbed both my wrists. This just gave me time and leverage to kick him hard in the shin above his boot. He let me go and bent over to rub his leg and I grabbed the hair on either side of his head and pulled his face so close to mine I could see spit freckling on his cheeks. Through gritted teeth, I snarled, "We'd all be better off without you."

He seized my wrists once more, pulling my hands off his hair. Dark brown strands were strung through my fingers. This time hurt, more than anything else, showed in his eyes. He heaved a sigh and said, "If you'd be so much better off without me, then maybe you ought to be the one to leave. Move in with your mama and daddy back in Gray Hampton. See how much better off you'd be there." He released my wrists and then clutched the back of a kitchen chair like he might have fallen over if he hadn't. "I'm going to bed, Sal. I can't take no more of this." He let go of the chair and lumbered out of the kitchen slumped and heavy like he had just been given bad news.

I followed him, flailing my arms: "What you mean is you can't stand to be around me, can you? I'm just a millstone around your neck, a hindrance to you. You think you're too good for a Skinner, don't you? Well, I'm not going anywhere, mister."

I started to follow him into the bedroom, but one time after we'd fought I'd been so worked up I ripped open his shirt, pushed him onto the bed, and climbed on top. Oil and water. This time, I grabbed a Coke and a pack of Viceroys and went outside. I paced the porch like that wild cat until my legs and my temper gave out. That was the meanest he'd ever been to me, and the harshest words he'd ever uttered. He knew I couldn't live in Gray Hampton and that I couldn't go back to being a Skinner. I sat down on the swing, leaned my head back, and closed my eyes. My ears pricked to the far-off and lonesome whistle of a late train.

I'd missed my period again, and still hadn't told Ivan. We'd only spoken when we had to since our fight. His job at the flourmill was scheduled to finish up tomorrow—marking the end of more than two years of backbreaking labor. "There'll be little more to do than clean up—besides a few finishing touches on the upper level."

He turned the volume down on the radio. "Is that all they can talk about, that damn *Ponder*." He was referring to the long shot that'd won the Derby last Saturday. He'd bet on the favorite, *Olympia*. She'd placed, but on a two-dollar bet, "It's hardly worth the bus fare to collect my winnings." Running late, he grabbed his lunch bucket, kissed us all, and raced out the door.

Rita dropped by later that day. She plopped herself down on the most substantial piece of furniture in the room. That couch creaked and groaned over her every word. I tried not to notice how it sagged from her weight. What Ivan's baby sister gave up in looks, she more than made up for in humor. She could get a hound dog to laugh. We had the best time talking about our kids and husbands, and telling dirty jokes.

Her Billy was a smallish man with hands and feet the size of a woman's. And Rita, she just got bigger with every baby. Ivan had told me they teased Billy at work that if Rita was ever on top, he'd never live to brag about it. It seemed to me that despite her size, Rita slid through life like she was greased. If she had problems, she didn't tell them.

I walked over and sat on the maroon couch next to her and was just about ready to confide that I was expecting again, when she got to the real reason she'd come.

"You should've heard Billy carrying on last night," she said as she slapped her thigh. "He was singing, 'we are gonna cut loose Fri-day night,' talking about the celebration that Wittenberg and Ballard's throwing for the men. Bill's wishing more for this job to be over than he is for Pee Wee and the Dodgers to win the pennant. I know Ivan must be too. He is going to the party tomorrow night, isn't he? They'll probably listen to the ballgame and start more rumors about the next assignment. Billy heard that the air board wants to add on to Standiford Field."

Rita talked a blue streak, like she was afraid to stop, and she had an unnatural look on her face like she was trying too hard to look natural. It all made me think that Ivan had put her up to it, coming over here trying to get me to okay him going to this party. I don't know if it was my condition or my anger, but I barely made it to the bathroom in time for the toilet to catch my lunch. Every smell was exaggerated. I could have sworn somebody was cooking cabbage.

Back in the living room I bent over to pick up the magazine that'd fallen off my lap when I was sent running. My stomach and my head still swam.

"Are you okay, Sal? I don't smell any cabbage."

"Well, maybe it's a rat I smell then." I said, picking invisible lint off the couch. "Was it Ivan or Billy who sent you over here to soften me up? If that's why you came, you'd just as well leave right now." I stood and walked to the back door to check on Nicole and Penny.

"Nobody put me up to nothing." Rita sounded hurt; she followed me with her eyes as I bustled from room to room. "I just thought you might not know about the party yet."

I rested against the doorway between the kitchen and living room and wiped my face with a cold washrag. "Doesn't it about kill you for Billy to go out like they do after work?"

"It's not like I want him to go," Rita squinted at me like I'd asked her how much she weighed. "But I don't really mind a time or two a week. He doesn't stay late and never comes home drunk. So, I figure what's the harm in him blowing off a little steam."

"Well, I can surely tell that you are Mr. Jim Barkley's daughter. Those are almost his exact words." I watched Rita use both fists to push herself up off the couch. It took two tries. I might have even seen a tear in her eye. She hooked her pocketbook over her arm and looked in every direction, except mine.

Then, her hand pushing open the front door, she paused and asked, "Is everybody else wrong and you're the only one right?" With that, Rita waddled off in as much of a huff as she could muster, and I wondered if Ivan would tell me about the party.

Out on the front porch later that afternoon, the girls snipped paper dolls out of the *McCall's* while I pulled weeds from a bed of fading daffodils. Nicole had Cyd Charisse and Penny dressed Fred Astaire in a tuxedo and tried to get the paper man to hold on to his cane. I looked up and spotted Ivan walking up the sidewalk. It was only the middle of May and his skin was already dark from working outside in the blazing Kentucky sun. It made his eyes show up like patches of blue in a stormy sky. He strode like he was carrying around something a lot heavier than that empty lunch box. I cut a handful of the daffodils and took them inside.

From the kitchen, I saw him open the door. He had a girl in each arm, with gangly ribbons of peach silk encircling his neck. He was Fred and the girls were Ginger and Cyd. He whirled them round and around the living room to giggles for music. They danced into the kitchen where I heard him take a deep breath. I hoped he was just sniffing the fried-chicken soaked air. I put a heaping bowl of dumplings on the table and pulled the coleslaw out of the Frigidaire.

"I smell fried chicken?" He said to his dance partners. "I swear your mama's the best cook there is."

I knew what he was doing. He was testing my mood, because, as he sat Penny in her highchair and Nicole in the one with the telephone book, he said, "I'm going to be running late tomorrow night.

Whittenberg and Ballard's buying burgers for the crew to celebrate after work."

He put a chicken leg on each girl's plate along with some slaw and dumplings. Penny whined about the slaw, so he scraped it onto his own dish. One time when I'd told Nicole to clean up her plate, I saw Ivan sneak bites to help her get rid of it. When Nicole giggled, he'd put his finger to his lips to shush her. He might as well have said: *You don't have to do what mama says.*

"I guess it was you who sent Rita over here today," I said. "So you can go out drinking Friday night with your real friends."

His mood was now as faded as that plot of yellow daffodils. "If Rita came over here today, she came because she wanted to visit and that's all," he said. "You know I'm going to be home all day for the next entire week, maybe more, until they give us our new assignment. I was thinking on the bus home about the two of us going out Saturday night for our own celebration—go to that Kaelin's Restaurant up in the Highlands? We could drop the girls off at Bill and Rita's for the night. That way, I can celebrate with the crew on Friday and we can have our own fun Saturday night—all the way to Sunday."

I wanted to believe he meant what he was saying but all I could think was that he was only trying to get me off his back—so he could go to Ott's without a fight.

I felt cold inside, like some maniac who kills people for the fun of it. First he sends Rita over here, and now he's trying to bribe me. He must really think I'm stupid, I thought.

Ivan sat down to take off his work boots. The girls came over to help with the laces.

"If you're done eating," I said, "go clean up your paper dolls." Nic and Penny scurried off, likely sensing that I was upset.

Those bluebell eyes focused their gaze on me for what felt like forever. Then, without blinking, he said, "I'm going to the celebration tomorrow night, Sal—you let me know if you want to go out on Saturday."

The girls came back in with armloads of magazines and shoeboxes of paper.

"It's only a matter of time before we find you passed out and peed on by some railroad tracks, anyway," I said. "Men are all the same." It was all I could do to keep from going after him, but I couldn't let the girls see me like that. I felt ashamed—ashamed that he would go to the celebration, knowing the way I felt, ashamed of how much I wanted to hurt him, and ashamed of who I was—Skinner trash.

"Let's take these to your room," Ivan said to Penny and Nicole, ignoring what I'd said to him. Afterwards the three of them cleaned up the dishes. He let them play in the dishwater, squeezing soapsuds through their hands and making sudsy mustaches and beards—something I never let them do.

I fixed myself a cold plate and eavesdropped on them from the front porch. I heard him ask them about their day—had they remembered to feed their dolls, were they the ones who'd fried the chicken, had they petted the kitty next door? He took his time and read each girl their favorite B'rer Rabbit story, and even stayed in their room until they fell asleep.

I heard him walk to the front door. I guess I should've turned around and looked at him or said something, or taken back my words. But, before I could say anything, I saw the light go on in the bedroom.

I waited for him to fall asleep before I went to bed. My side was already turned down when I crawled in after midnight. He wasn't breathing like he was asleep. I felt mad and sorry all at the same time. I thought about a time four years back when we'd gone to the movies with Billy and Rita. We had held hands on the bus there and through the whole show at the Ohio Theater. We watched *The African Queen* with Katharine Hepburn and Humphrey Bogart. Ivan had always told me he thought I looked like Katharine Hepburn.

In the wood-carved Brown Hotel bar afterwards, we had a time drinking beers and cokes and eating burgers. The four of us were talking about how Miss Priss Kate had gotten all wet and muddy in that river, and Ivan had told us a story about when the army had sent him to Alaska to work on the Alcan Highway. In the spring when the weather warmed up, the ground had thawed and turned to mush almost a foot deep. At the end of the workday, they'd have mud in places you'd never dream mud could get.

"I thought I'd be smart and asked my buddy, Foster, if I could borrow his extra pair of boots," Ivan said. "I told him mine were about to wear through. Truth was I just wanted to give them a chance to dry out. The leather never dried all the way overnight.

"Well, it turned out Foster was a size twelve and here I am a nine. So the entire day every time I'd take a step, damned if that slushy mud didn't suck those boots right off my feet, first one, and then the other. I ended up spending more time on my butt than my feet—muddy and soppy as old Kate."

We hooted and howled at how Ivan's trick had backfired on him. He was never ashamed to tell on himself, especially if it got a laugh.

Maybe I should have awakened him and told him I was sorry about what I'd said. I knew he wasn't a bad man. But I wasn't sure if I'd be able to stand it if he went to Ott's on Friday night.

The next morning while he got ready for work, I fixed his lunch—cold chicken and a thermos of tea—and put it in his lunch box. He tied up his work boots and planted his regular goodbye kisses on Nicole's and Penny's foreheads before heading out the front door and on to the bus stop on Broadway.

I followed to watch him go. He bent over to open the gate latch, and then straightened up like somebody had called his name. He walked back toward the house, and I hurried back into the kitchen.

"Poppy!" Penny gurgled, her mouth full of milk.

"Forgot my cigarettes," he said, stuffing a fresh pack of Viceroys into his shirt pocket.

I bit my lip hard to keep from saying anything ugly.

He walked over to the sink and put a palm on either side of my waist. I got those same shivers like the day he'd boosted me up on Demon. I smelled his Halo shampoo and Old Spice. His warm lips bussed my cheek, then he headed off again.

In unison, the girls trilled, "Bye bye, Poppy," and I waited for the front door to slam.

Later, the girls were playing in the backyard, searching for new places to hide from the ragman who drove his horse cart up our alley every Friday afternoon. Nicole and Penny would lie in the grass on their bellies waiting and listening for the *clip-clop, clip-clop, clip-clop* of the two swayback grays on the brick alley. At the first sound, they'd scream and hide behind bushes or trees, then peek around to see him. They were fascinated by the spirited, deep-voiced colored man who boomed out his own name over and over. "Ragman," he would roar, making it sound more like prayer when he'd sing it slow and low, "RRRRaagmon," like a spiritual from *Porgy and Bess.*

I'd settled into a stuffed chair in the living room with my bare feet resting on the ottoman, drinking a Coca-Cola, smoking my Viceroy, and searching through the JC Penney catalog. The girls needed summer shoes and I was going to need a couple of new dresses—maternity dresses. I'd decided to tell Ivan tonight that I was expecting again. He would be so excited. After Penny, he'd said if we ever had another girl, he wanted to name her Heddy, after his grandmother. The way that man loved kids could sometimes make everything wrong about him seem right.

I heard their footsteps and smelled the familiar sweat and sawdust before I saw them. I breathed in the scent, the smell of Ivan. "Well, look what the cat dragged in. You all get done early?" I said as I turned toward the odor. Billy had pulled open the screen door and I could see the foreman coming up behind him. I was so tickled they'd come to my house instead of going to Ott's, that I didn't even say anything about them wearing their dusty boots indoors.

I pulled myself out of the chair to go to the kitchen to fetch four Falls City beers—for the celebration. That was when Billy laid his hand on my arm. He motioned toward the chair and told me to sit back down. His brown eyes were red and swollen.

"What for?" I asked, feeling a little worried by the look of his eyes and by an unfamiliar crack in his voice. "Where's Ivan?" I looked past him to see if my husband was in sight.

"There's been a fall," Billy said. "Sit back down there; I've got some real bad news." He put his palms together like he might be asking for help, and then he looked square at me. "Ivan's gone, Sal."

I staggered and the foreman took my hand and helped me to the chair.

"You're not funny, Billy Crawley. He's not gone. Now, stop it!" I said.

"I'd never joke like that. It's so, Sal"

"Then you tell me . . . how a man like Ivan could fall."

Billy seemed like he was trying to stay calm; taking deep breaths. "We ate lunch together like always. Ivan had to trade his fried chicken for one of the Protestant's grilled cheese sandwiches. We laughed at how you keep forgetting that he can't eat meat on Fridays. Afterwards, we headed back up the inside ladder to the top of the silo. The foreman picked us to bolt the last cap on the last silo."

I knew not to fix him meat on Fridays. The girls and I were always careful, but I couldn't seem to remember about his lunches since I always fixed them on Thursday night.

Billy paused. "Keep going," I said.

"Ivan saw it first. The crew before us had left their walk board up there, which was a serious code violation. It was what they'd used to get back and forth across the top of the open shaft. Ivan pointed to it and told me to watch out, that it wasn't nailed down.

"I told him I saw it and turned around to pull up the bucket of bolts we needed for the cap."

Billy started to cry, but I made him keep telling it. The foreman had squatted beside my chair and was patting my hand.

"Then, Lord help me, Sal, the next thing I heard was the sound of something smacking against the silo. I wheeled around and saw that Ivan had stepped on the outside part of that board—on the part that hung over the edge. I can't figure how he did it, after he'd just warned me about being careful of it." Billy stared off like he was watching it happen again. "He fell, Sal. Looking down at him from the top of the silo, he looked like a child laying there on the ground—the way kids sometimes curl up funny when they fall asleep."

Billy knelt down on the other side of my chair; he pulled a handkerchief out of his pocket and handed it to me. "I dread telling Rita," he said, rubbing his forehead, "and Mr. Jim."

I wove the handkerchief in and out of my fingers.

I looked at Billy again to make sure he wasn't lying to me—but his face told me the truth. Feeling angry and betrayed, I tried to think of somebody to blame. I twisted and twirled that bandana as Mr. Jim's old threat that "there'd be hell to pay" echoed in my mind alongside Billy's words.

"So, it was an accident." I emphasized the "was" to keep from sounding like I was asking a question.

The foreman finally spoke up. "The men are already being questioned about what they saw, but Bill, here was the only one on the silo with Ivan when he fell and he had his back to him. Ivan would've had to step out on the overhanging part of that board deliberately for it not to be. So, yes, it will be ruled an accident."

"Sal," Billy said. "I'll talk to Mr. Jim about making the arrangements in Gray Hampton."

"Gray Hampton." I knew the voice I heard was mine, but the sound of it was flat and cold like those World War II soldiers when they came home from the war; the ones they called shell-shocked.

I heard their voices, but I didn't care—not about Bill's or the foreman's, nor the girls' cries, the ragman's call, nor anything else. I just kept saying the name of that place, the one that Ivan had rescued me from, uttering it over and over, maybe to hear my voice again or maybe to bear out the truth of it.

I chewed the skin on my lower lip, not satisfied until I tasted blood. "Gray Hampton."

From the backyard, little girl squeals sweetly sifted through the screen door like sugar crystals tinkling into a fine china cup.

Hooves clip-clopped up the alley. “RRRRaagmon,” the old man chanted.

BABY BLUES

Somehow Mama managed to wait until after the baby came to have her nervous breakdown—even though she'd threatened it every single day since Poppy's accident. At only seven years old, I still did everything I could to keep my sister, Penny, out of her way because it never took much to set Mama off.

Our cousin Bernice, from Gray Hampton, had been living with us while she studied hair styling and color at the Louisville School of Beauty. This turned out to be a really a good thing, because if she hadn't been there when Mama broke down, who knows what would have happened.

It was Bernice who carried Heddy into the kitchen that December morning in 1949. "Here's the birthday girl—one whole month old." Mama was brewing a pot of coffee and I was helping Penny, who was five, tie her shoes.

Mama stuffed a paper grocery sack with trash and set it on the floor next to the back door.

Penny started singing *Happy Birthday to Heddy*, but I told her that a one-month birthday wasn't old enough for the birthday song.

"Morning Sal," Bernice said as she scuffed across the linoleum. No matter what she said, it always made me want to snicker. It wasn't that Bernice was funny, but the way she sounded when she spoke or laughed was hilarious. While her mouth formed the consonants and vowels of words, it seemed like all the talk came out through her nose, sending forth a wail as shrill and ear-piercing as a merry-go-round needing to be greased. Mama said that Bernice could have been a movie star, if it wasn't for that nasally voice of hers.

When Mama poured the coffee, Bernice lifted her chin off her fist and crooked her head toward her—she'd probably noticed the way she was dressed.

"Is this going to be a dress-up day?" I thought this because Mama had put on baggy jeans, one of Poppy's shirts that hung to her knees, and she had draped a long yellow scarf around her head and neck, like the ladies in her movie star magazines. I thought maybe she was feeling better and might want to play with us today.

But Mama didn't answer me. She just sat a coffee mug on the table in front of Bernice, and picked Heddy up out of Bernice's lap. She walked to the back door where she'd sat the sack of trash earlier, opened the door and carried Heddy out into the cold. Mama laid her tiny bundle down on an icy metal chair where she usually sat the garbage until she had time to carry it to the alley. She walked back inside straight to the kitchen sink like she didn't even hear Heddy squalling her head off.

Bernice shot out of her chair so fast that she dumped her coffee all over the floor; for which she got an awfully dirty look. Mama grabbed a drying towel and began mopping up the mess, seeming oblivious to the goings-on.

"What's wrong with you?" Bernice screamed as she ran to the porch. She scooped up the wailing infant and hurried back indoors with Heddy wrapped inside her robe. All our eyes were on Mama, following her around the room as she cleaned up the spill, poured two more cups of coffee, and sat down at the table.

"Sal, are you okay?" Bernice tipped a bottle into Heddy's mouth and when Mama didn't respond, she said, "Nicole, run and call Rita and Billy and tell them they need to get over here." Aunt Rita was Poppy's sister and Uncle Billy was her husband.

I grabbed Penny's hand and ran to the living room where I dialed the number I knew by heart.

"Bernice says you and Uncle Billy better get over here, right now," I said into the black mouthpiece. "Mama's not talking."

For two days Mama had hardly spoken to either Penny or me. She sat at the kitchen table or paced most of the day. The night before, she came into Penny's and my room twice, asking us if we'd seen Poppy. She said something about her sister that sounded like, "Gladys can't have you back." She wasn't making any sense. I remember feeling glad that Penny hadn't woken up. Mama emptied out her chest of drawers all over the floor of her bedroom and I heard her counting, "Eight socks, two pairs of hose, three nightgowns, seven pairs of shoes, six blouses, one rug."

This morning Mama's eyes were hopping from thing to thing, as if she was watching a fly circle and light, circle and light. I couldn't trail what she was looking at. It seemed like her mind might have been following her eyes because she could not sit still either. She'd sit down, then get up and walk to the sink, turn on the water, come back and sit down and then do it all again.

When Uncle Billy and Aunt Rita got to our house and heard what all Mama had been doing, Aunt Rita asked Bernice if she would stay with Penny and Heddy and me. She said she thought Mama needed to see a doctor. They tricked her into getting in their car by telling her they were taking her to White Castle for breakfast.

"Is Ivan going too?" Mama asked as she scooted across the seat.

"He's meeting us there."

I looked at Bernice to see why Uncle Billy had said that, because Poppy died months before when he fell off the grain silo he was building. "Is Poppy still dead?" I asked.

Bernice hugged my head against her side and held Penny on the other. "Your uncle was just trying not to upset your mother even more." It wasn't long after Mama and Uncle Billy told us Poppy had been killed, that Mama let us know we were having another baby.

Still leaning against Bernice, Penny pulled her thumb out of her mouth long enough to ask, "Can we go to White Castle, too?"

Bernice led us into the kitchen. "Let's fix you girls some cereal."

When I sat down at the table, I realized that I had peed my pants. I didn't say anything to Bernice. Seven-year-olds were not supposed to wet themselves. I was so afraid that I would never see Mama again. That's the way it happened with Poppy. He went to work one day and never came home. He kissed both our foreheads and said, "Bye Penny, bye Nickle." He teased me sometimes and called me Nickle, I guess he was making a joke because my sister's name was Penny. My real name is Nicole. I used to get so mad at him for calling me a name that was only worth five cents.

Bernice laid Heddy back in her bassinette. It seemed like all that baby could do was sleep or eat or cry.

"When's Mama coming back?" I asked. "Where did they take her?"

I gazed at Mama's coffee cup that was still sitting on the table. I knew it was hers because of the red lipstick on the rim.

"I figure they took her to Our Lady of Peace Hospital. It's a place where she can get some rest. Your Poppy's passing, and this new baby has put a terrible strain on her."

Bernice played with Penny and me all day when she wasn't tending to Heddy. She read to us and we played hide and seek.

It was after three o'clock when Aunt Rita and Uncle Billy came back, without Mama. They promised us that she would come home in two weeks and that she would be feeling a lot better. Then they packed up our clothes and drove Penny, Heddy, and me to Mama's mother's house in Gray Hampton.

Mama hated Gray Hampton, the town where she was raised. She was always telling us what an awful place it was and how lucky we were to live in a nice town like Louisville.

□

The first thing Mama did when she got out of the hospital was sell our house to the neighbor, and buy another one in Gray Hampton. When she finally came to get us at Mam's, she told us that everything from our Louisville house had been moved into the new one at 313 Magnolia Street.

"This is my worst nightmare," I heard Mama tell Mam as she cuddled the baby she hadn't seen in almost three weeks. "Coming back to this hell hole. Where is Daddy, anyway?" Then she made her mouth crooked and said, "Like I have to ask."

They talked, and Penny and I listened while we jammed our clothes into paper sacks to take to our new house. Mama said that her daddy drank too much whiskey and that he was mean to Mam. She said that everybody in Gray Hampton thought the Skinners were no good. But I knew she couldn't mean Mam. Mam sang hymns and said her prayers even if she didn't go to church.

"Let's go, Mama, I want to see my house." Penny jumped up and down like a baby kangaroo.

I held Heddy on my lap for the short drive. It couldn't have taken more than about three minutes. Mama said it was a small town.

I was careful to watch for what kind of mood Mama was in so I could keep Penny and Heddy from lighting her fuse. Penny said that she thought Mama glowed red when she was mad and blue when she was sad. She said she could see the color all around her. But when she went pale white and wouldn't talk, we were afraid we would have to call Aunt Rita again or Mam. But since she'd come home from the hospital, those moods never lasted long. Mostly she acted sleepy, not busy like before. And all she talked about was finding a way to move back to Louisville.

A few weeks after we moved, Bernice dropped by to see our house and to play with Penny and Heddy and me. She brought her Beauty School diploma with her to show us. She asked Mama how she liked the new house.

"It'll do, I guess, it wasn't like I had much choice?"

Bernice played patty cake with Heddy and winked at Penny and me, peeking at her from either side of a chair.

"What do you think of the color of my hair?" Bernice poofed the stylish bob with her palms. "It's called *champagne*."

Mama looked at her like she was making herself do it. "You look real nice Bernice, you always do. Congratulations on finishing school." Mama ran her fingers through her own hair like she might do before answering the doorbell.

Mama examined her chewed fingernails that before Poppy died were always filed and polished bright red. She tapped her chair for Penny to come sit next to her. The chair was fitted with a green nubby slipcover with pink and cream cabbage roses on it that Mama said "perfectly accented" her maroon couch. She'd spent hours picking out the material for it and then sewing it. But she didn't seem to be as proud of her things as she had once been. She hadn't bothered to arrange the furniture or even clean house since we'd moved in.

"I've got a job interview next week at Farmer's Bank. I thought

Ivan's papa might offer me a few dollars, so I could put off having to go to work until Heddy was at least six months, but he hasn't spoken to me since the funeral except to ask if he can take Penny here and there."

Mr. Jim Barkley, Poppy's papa, didn't seem to like Mama very much. One time I heard him tell Poppy he thought she was too feisty.

"I had to use most of the insurance money to bury Ivan."

Bernice was barely listening. She was squirmy like she had an itch she was trying not to scratch. Then, she interrupted Mama right in the middle of her telling how mean Papa Jim had been to her at Poppy's funeral.

"Okay, I wasn't going to tell anybody until I told Mommy, but I can't wait any longer," Bernice held Heddy over her head like a stuffed doll she'd won at the fair. "I might be getting married! Hootie Chadwick proposed last night. I haven't answered him yet, but I'm almost positive I want to." She giggled and snorted out her nose and looked sheep-eyed at Mama.

"Isn't he that youngest Chadwick boy? The one who spends most of his time and money in the Flaherty bars?" Mama did not like for men to go out drinking in bars. She and Poppy used to have awful fights when he'd come home from a tavern.

"He's the youngest, but I wouldn't say he spends much of his time in the bars. You don't want cousin Bernice to be an old maid, do you?" Bernice cooed to Heddy. "Besides, I want me one of these." She kissed the kicking and squirming baby.

Mama hugged Penny and kissed her white hair. "I don't know what I'd do without my girls, but there are worse things than being an old maid."

"You're not old, Mama." Penny looked back at her.

"You're only eighteen, Bernice, you've got time." Then she softened her eyes a little and said; "Don't let him put you in some Flaherty shack. You've seen that dump he was raised in, looks like two trailers shoved together." Flaherty was just one town over, but was in another county, a "wet" district, which is why Mama had such an attitude about it. Gray Hamptoners complained about the Flaherty bars, but many of its men could be found at Shorty's Liquors or Brown's Tavern on Friday and Saturday nights.

Bernice bit her bottom lip and pouted like she might be about to cry. "I ought to go," she said, coughing and eyeing her watch. "I told Mommy I'd help her cook tonight." She put Heddy down on her blanket and gave her forehead another kiss.

"You could move in here if you just want to get away from home," Mama said. "There's a nice apartment in the basement."

Mama shook her head and scowled as she watched Bernice walk out the door. I wondered why the idea of her marrying Hootie upset Mama so much. Was she afraid that Hootie Chadwick might die like Poppy, or maybe that he'd be mean like Daddy Skinner?

Penny plopped down on Heddy's blanket. She shook a pink plastic rattle just out of the baby's reach. Mama walked over to the picture window and stared out.

"That's all people in this town expect of a woman—marry some lazy drunk, have his babies and put up with his guff the rest of her life." It seemed more like Mama was talking to herself than us.

"Well, that won't be the way it is with me. I won't give them the satisfaction." Mama stepped back from the glass and folded her arms. She was inspecting the window now, instead of looking through it. "As soon as I get my first paycheck, I'm buying us some curtains." Penny and I laughed because Mama held her nose when she said it, making her voice sound twangy like Bernice's.

When Mama came to pick us up at Mam's after her job interview, she was all smiles.

"What kind of a job is it?" Daddy Skinner asked. "Cleaning houses? Washing clothes?" He banged his pipe on the metal ashtray that stood on a pedestal next to his chair. Brown ashes and burnt tobacco fell out of the bowl. His pipe made the house smell sweet, like cherries. Sometimes the smell was so strong it would make my stomach ache.

Mama gave him a hateful look. She jerked her eyes away and hurried into the kitchen where she knew she'd find Mam. Penny and I followed like baby ducks.

"I got a job at the bank, Mama." She grinned and clasped her hands in front of her blue straight skirt like a little girl.

"The bank!" Mam was wide-eyed. "How in the wide world did you get a job there?" She dropped a ham hock into a pot of navy beans.

"Maybe, I'm not as dumb as some people think." She curled her upper lip and cocked her eyes toward the front room.

A voice said, "Maybe, it's because your name ends in Barkley instead of Skinner."

Mam grabbed Mama's arm to stop her from charging at him. "He's not worth it," Mam whispered.

Mama always said that the Barkleys had money. She said it was probably because they didn't drink it up in taverns.

When we left Mam's, we went directly to St. George's grade school where Mama registered Penny for kindergarten and me in first grade. I'd missed a lot of school since Mama had been sick. But I was excited to be going back.

We stopped at Perry Hardware and bought a metal sign that said "Apartment for Rent."

When we got home, Mama said, "Nicole, watch the baby a minute." And she went outside and hung the sign under the mailbox.

Even with a good job and a renter in her basement apartment, Mama still fell quiet occasionally. She would look like she might be trying to remember, or maybe forget something, but her face and eyes stayed soft. Penny called these moods baby blue, because Mama wasn't mad and she wasn't crying, just sort of dreamy. Sometimes she would want to hug us more and sit close to us and tell us stories about Poppy or about when we were babies. Penny and I looked forward to these times. It made me feel the way I used to when I'd wake up from a nap and the sun would be shining on my bed and I could hear Mama and Poppy talking in soft voices in the next room.

Mama said she had what she called a "feel sorry" for each one of us. She liked to tell us the stories that went along with the "feel sorry," and Penny and I loved to listen to them. The only problem was that she would only tell Penny and Heddy's stories. She'd never tell mine.

One evening we were sitting at the supper table, when Mama said, "Lets all go sit in the living room." I looked over at Penny who was already eyeing me. We started to clear the table but Mama said to leave it.

I pulled Heddy out of her high chair and carried her into the living room where Mama and Penny were already curled up on the couch.

"My poor little Penny," I heard Mama whimper into my little sister's ear. "We came so close to losing you."

"Tell my story Mama, Heddy and Nicole want to hear it too." We all snuggled tight against Mama. Penny was close to celebrating her seventh birthday and I was going on nine. Heddy was almost two and a half, but even she seemed to like listening to the stories.

Mama ran her hand across the nylon nap of the maroon couch. It was her prized possession, and it wasn't often that she allowed us to sit on it.

"You were only eight months old when you spiked an awful fever. It was Sunday night and you were so sick you didn't even cry."

Penny sat up straight and turned her face toward Mama. "I think I was trying to be brave." Penny wrinkled her brow and looked earnest.

Mama told us that when she and Poppy got Penny to the hospital and the nun took her temperature, it read 105º. "Boy did they start to scramble. Dr. McAuliffe was called in and Poppy and I got sent to sit in a big room where we had to wait and wait."

Mama took the bottle out of Heddy's mouth and sat it on the floor. "Don't let me forget that."

She said that I fell asleep in Poppy's lap for almost two hours. When the doctor finally came into the waiting room, he was frowning and looked tired and he took hold of Mama's hand.

She looked serious like she was imitating him.

" 'It's not good,' " Mama quoted the Doc, " 'she's got viral meningitis. Even if we pull her through this, she's going to have problems. Her fever was too high for too long.' "

Penny and I peeked at each another, but stayed quiet so as not to break Mama's spell. Heddy sucked her thumb and fingered the silky part of her blanket while she slept.

Poppy started to cry so hard, Mama continued to explain, that she had to grab me off his lap before he dropped me on my head. "I told him we don't need two sick babies."

"By Friday, nothing had changed. Poppy and I sat in the hospital cafeteria, him with his face in his hands, sobbing like a baby. All you had done for a solid week was sleep."

I knew Penny was trying to keep quiet, but she couldn't help herself. "Were you mad at me, Mama?"

"Course not," Mama said. "When we went back upstairs to wait for the doctor to come, Poppy walked into your room ahead of me. And there you were, pulled up against the prison bars of that baby bed, wearing nothing but your diaper, and grinning like I don't know what. Then you reached your arms out and said, "Poppy." I screamed, causing the entire staff to come running. I'm telling you there wasn't a dry eye in the room—Doc McAuliffe, the nun-nurse, Poppy, nor me. Penny was the only one laughing. Just goes to show you, doctors don't know everything."

I could tell by the grin on her face that Penny loved hearing how she'd outwitted everybody.

"Don't put your feet on the coffee table, Nic." Mama patted my knee. She kept on telling how we hadn't been able to bring Penny home until the next Sunday, and by that time, "it was like you'd never been sick." The doctor said to take your temperature everyday that week, but he hadn't even sent you home with medicine.

"What's meningitis, Mama?"

"It's an infection on the brain," Penny said, looking all puffed up like Miss Smarty Britches.

Mama stood up, still holding Heddy. "I need to put this baby to bed." She tiptoed toward the hall.

"Were you and Poppy glad that I didn't catch it?"

Looking back at me, Mama said they had been really worried that I might get it. "But Doc said you would've shown symptoms by the time Penny came home. He'd seen several cases and knew just what to do. He put the rest of us on some kind of pills that were supposed to keep us well."

When Mama was out of sight, I stuck my tongue out at Penny for being such a wiseacre, but she just laughed. Mama came back to the couch, put her head back, closed her eyes, and sighed like she was tired. "I just hope none of us gets sick in this place. Here it is nineteen fifty-two and there's no hospital close and nothing but country doctors to see. As soon as I make enough money, we're moving back to Louisville. This is no place to raise kids."

"I like it here, Mama. We get to see Mam and our cousins. All three of us like it here fine." I leaned over close to Mama and held her hand. "Tell my 'feel sorry' now, please, you never tell mine."

Mama rubbed my hand. "Not tonight Nic, maybe next time."

It was what she always said. I folded my arms across my chest and sat back on the couch hard. But Mama didn't seem to notice. I wasn't sure what had made her get all worked up so quick, but she jumped up from the couch so fast that Penny and I fell against each other like dominoes.

"Everything fell apart when Ivan died," Mama strode around the room, and then looked back at Penny and me and frowned.

"It's okay, Mama, it's nice here," Penny said.

"What was I supposed to do?" Mama started to cry and wipe her forehead.

Mama wasn't talking to us anymore, so I told Penny to say "goodnight" and we went to our bedroom. "Do you think we ought to do the dishes?" I asked Penny. "I'm afraid it'll make too much noise and make Mama mad."

Penny shrugged her shoulders and started to change into her pajamas.

"Why do you think Mama won't ever tell my story? She says she has a 'feel sorry' for me too."

"She said maybe next time she would," Penny buttoned her cotton top.

"That's what she always says and then she tells yours or Heddy's." I couldn't figure it out. I was starting to think that maybe she just hadn't come up with one yet or maybe she didn't care about me as much as she did Penny and Heddy. "He ruined everything," I heard Mama wail.

I turned out the light and pushed the door closed.

Sometimes, Papa Jim would invite Penny to spend the night at his house with Gram and him, but only Penny. "Why can't I go too?" I asked.

"Mr. Jim is just partial to Penny, I guess."

Penny would come home with books and toys that she'd share, but she made sure we knew they were hers. One time after Sunday Mass, Mama tried to have a talk with Papa Jim outside of church. "Ivan wouldn't think much of how you treat Heddy and Nicole. That baby is your flesh and blood, too."

Papa Jim sort of looked down his nose at her and turned around and headed for his car, brushing her off like she was a gnat or a fly.

Mama had her hand on her hip like she was trying to look tough while she stood there watching him walk away. Penny and I held on to Heddy's hands. We stood at the bottom of the church steps and waited.

Out of the blue, Papa Jim wheeled around and stormed back toward Mama. She didn't even flinch. He put his pointer finger in her face and said, "Listen here Sal Skinner, no woman tells me what's what. My business is mine and you'd just better stay out of it, if you know what's good for you."

Gram was standing by their car. "Jim, I need to get home, I've got a roast in the oven."

As Papa Jim began walking away again, Mama said, "The name's Barkley, just like yours." Then she flipped around so fast that her skirt twirled like a dancer's, showing her white crinolines. Her face, especially her eyes, were as fierce as a lion's. I hadn't seen her look like that since we'd moved to Gray Hampton.

We'd walked to St. George's that Sunday. Once Mama got us across the street she sped on ahead of us, taking strides so long she was almost running. I knew she was probably about to cry and didn't want anybody to see her. We took it slow and even played outside a while to give Mama time to calm down.

The only Barkley relatives we got to see outside of church were our Aunts Aggie and Rita. The Saturday after Labor Day, when I'd just started fourth grade Poppy's two sisters pulled their sedan into our driveway.

I opened the car door and five cousins piled out. We all laughed and ran off to play in the backyard. Aunt Rita had brought school dresses for Penny and me that her Marilyn and Margaret Marie had outgrown.

We played *Mother May I*, *Red Rover*, and *Hide-n-Seek*. There were better places to hide here than in Louisville. This yard rolled like a pasture and had as many trees as a forest. The front yard had grass that Mama mowed, but the back was shady, mossy, and damp, with acorns, whole and shelled, spread all over the ground. The dogwoods were just beginning to change color, their berries turning from green to red.

After we finished a sweaty game of tag, everybody said they wanted to see baby Heddy. So I went in through the basement to get her. I walked up the stairs as quietly as I could and stopped at the top to listen for a minute. I could see that Mama had put out a plate of her homemade bourbon balls that she'd saved in the freezer since last Christmas. She'd put on a pot of coffee and sat three pink-flowered plates on the gray and white Formica kitchen table.

My aunts were oohing and ahhing over Heddy. My ears perked up when I heard Aggie say my name.

"Nicole has always been the picture of your family, Sal, and Penny is every bit a Barkley. But I believe Heddy is an equal mixture of the Skinners and the Barkleys. Don't you think so, Rita? Look at those green eyes. It's a shame she never got to know her daddy (which happened to be Mama's "feel sorry" for Heddy). Billy and Tommy are fine men, but Ivan outshined them both when it came to being a father. I couldn't get Tommy to change a diaper if his life depended on it."

"Billy neither." Rita chimed in.

Aggie lit a cigarette and held the match up for Heddy to blow out. Heddy formed her rosebud mouth into a perfect "O." But no matter how hard she blew, the match continued its red and yellow jig until Aggie, laughing, shook the flames away.

The sisters continued to talk about Poppy between bites of candy and cooing with Heddy. I was about to step into the kitchen when I heard my name again.

Aunt Rita started to brag about how good Poppy had been to me. "Treated her just like she was his own daughter," she said—and how he never showed any partiality to Penny.

I wondered what she meant. Why wouldn't he treat me like his daughter? Even though I was starting to itch from sweat and from confusion, I thought I'd better stay and listen.

Mama popped a bourbon ball in her mouth and got up to pour more coffee. I could see her cheeks starting to glow pink.

"I've yet to know a man that was half as good a father as Ivan," Mama said.

I watched her pull back the café curtains to check on us.

"Where's Nicole?" She dropped the curtain and headed for the door.

"I'm here, Mama," I muttered from the top of the basement stairs. "I came in to get Heddy." I slid into the kitchen like I hadn't paused for even a second. "Want to go outside and see your cousins?" She climbed out of her chair and ran past me to the door.

"Sugar, you have Marilyn help you watch that baby." Aunt Rita was referring to her oldest daughter. I elbowed the back door open and led Heddy down the concrete steps.

I could see all three women gawking out the window as I sat down in a lawn chair with Heddy. Marilyn ran right over. The others had raked up a giant pile of leaves and were jumping in it and burying each other. Heddy ran over to the pile and leaped right on top of Penny. Everybody fell down laughing.

I couldn't keep my mind on our games anymore. All I could think about was what I'd just heard my aunts say. I turned it over and over in my brain.

Then I remembered something that had happened at school last spring. My creepy cousin, Kenny Skinner, wouldn't quit teasing me. He'd said, "You're about as much a Barkley as my dog."

I told him to shut up and leave me alone or I was going to tell. Then he said, "Where do think you got all those freckles? I bet they're on your butt, too." I started to chase him, and he ran away.

When I got home from school I went into the bathroom and stared at my face full of freckles. I pulled my pants down and craned my neck to see my backside. Sure enough, there were freckles all over my bottom. How would creepy Kenny Skinner know that, when I hadn't even known it?

After supper, I asked Mama, "How come I've got so many

freckles? Penny and Heddy don't have any." Mama said she thought freckles ran on her side of the family.

"You kids come in here and wash your face and hands. We got to get home." Aunt Aggie hollered.

I grabbed Heddy and followed the others inside. Aunt Rita supervised the scrubbing. Then as we filed past Mama on our way back outdoors, she handed each one of us half a Popsicle; probably to cut down on the fussing over them having to leave. The cousins pinched Heddy's cheeks and pecked her goodbye with sweet orange mouths before scooting five across in the backseat of the Ford.

Back in the house, I was about to ask Mama about what I'd heard the aunts say, when I noticed that she had turned the color of dogwood berries. Instead, I suggested that Penny, Heddy, and I take our baths before supper.

Mama must have started fixing supper because Penny had to jump out of the tub and throw up in the toilet. She couldn't stand the smell of boiled hot dogs. After our baths, when we sat around the kitchen table, nobody complained about the food. It looked like Mama had boiled the life out of those wieners. Both ends of every one had exploded like firecrackers, pink fringe with white innards.

I cut Heddy's food into little bites and kept the plate on the table until it was cool enough for her to eat. Penny smothered her bun with mustard and ketchup and relish to try and bury the taste and stink, as well as her misery. When we finished our silent dinner,

Penny collected all the paper plates. She wrapped them in newspaper and carried the waste to the metal garbage can in the driveway so she wouldn't have to smell them any longer.

We took Heddy to our room to play a game of Candyland.

"They just can't seem to stay out of my business." Mama mumbled in the kitchen still slamming pots and cabinet doors. "Damn them."

Around 7:30 she came into our room. "Time for bed Heddy, girl." Heddy's crib was in Mama's bedroom.

When Penny and I heard Heddy ask for water and a story, we held our breath for fear that she would fan Mama's fire.

Mama read Heddy the story of the three pigs. Even after we heard Heddy breathing like she did when she was asleep, Mama kept reading until the little pigs had finished building their indestructible brick house.

Penny and I saw Mama walk past our door toward the living room where she sat on the couch. She lowered her chin and rested it against her chest for more than fifteen minutes. She went to the kitchen where it sounded like she heated up that afternoon's coffee in a pan, and then poured it into her cup. She carried the cup back to the couch where she scarfed down the one remaining bourbon ball.

Penny and I jumped like rabbits when Mama spoke. "Nicole Marie, come here."

Penny asked if she could come too. "I want to talk to Nicole by herself tonight, you go on to bed. If you want you can leave the light on and read your book until Nic comes back."

Mama patted the couch for me to sit next to her. I wasn't sure if I was in trouble for eavesdropping that afternoon or what. Mama never talked to us separately.

She was quiet a minute and took a breath so deep her shoulders shrugged from the effort. Then she said, "I'm going to tell you your story, Nic; it's the reason why I feel sorry for you. I'm ashamed I didn't tell it to you sooner. Poppy and I wanted to, but I guess we just waited too long. So, here it is."

I slid into the corner of the couch and drew my feet up tight. I tucked my knees under my chin, afraid and excited at the same time. "Why can't Penny and Heddy hear it too?"

"I thought you might want to hear it by yourself first in case you have some questions." Then she started.

"Poppy and I'd been married for almost three years and were starting to think that maybe we weren't going to have children. We both wanted kids, but I'd accepted the fact that maybe we wouldn't. Not Poppy, he loved kids so much he was even willing to adopt a baby from an orphanage if we had to."

Mama got up off the couch and marched the floor. The worried look on her face made me think this was going to be a bad story.

"About that same time, Mam told us that my little sister, Gladys, was going to have a baby. She wasn't married and still lived with Mam and Daddy Skinner, and it wouldn't be easy for her to raise a child by herself.

"Poppy and I talked it over for a month or more and we agreed that when you were born, we'd talk to Gladys about her letting us have you."

I looked square at Mama. Was she saying that Aunt Gladys was my mother? Mama wasn't my real mother? I was confused. I wanted Mama to hush so I could go be with Penny; read our books together and never have to hear my story. I didn't like what she was saying.

"You were born right in Mam Skinner's front bedroom on a Saturday night. Poppy and I waited a week before we went to see you. I talked to Mam first about our idea of adopting you and she thought it would be okay to bring it up to Gladys. So Poppy and I went in the bedroom to talk to her."

Mama continued to circle the room. But she kept looking at me like she might be trying to catch me at something.

"At first Gladys said we couldn't have you, that she wanted to raise her baby. But I reminded her how mean our drunken daddy used to be to us as kids; then Mam talked to her for a while and got her to change her mind."

Mama sat back down next to me and turned so she could look at me straight on.

"Then Gladys gave you about twenty kisses and you and Poppy and I left, fighting over who got to hold you and who would drive. You've been with us ever since and I'm as glad of it as a mother can be.

"So that's your story. Ask me anything you want to."

I didn't know what to say or ask. I was too stunned to think. I felt myself starting to cry. "Does everybody know Aunt Gladys is my mother?" Mama handed me a tissue and I wiped my nose. I got a new one and dabbed at my eyes, and I thought about how some of the Skinner cousins called Aunt Gladys, "Glad Ass" to be mean.

"Grown-ups in the family know, but that ought to be all." She was sitting right next to me, but it felt like she'd drifted a hundred miles away. "Poppy and I tried to get Gladys to sign papers so we could adopt you, but she never would."

Mama put her hands under my arms and sat me in her lap like a baby. She hugged me and rubbed my head just like I was her true daughter.

"Is that why Aunt Gladys always comes to see us when she comes home, and why she sends me those post cards?" Aunt Gladys had lived in California with her husband for as long as I could remember. Mama nodded and then it occurred to me that Poppy must not be my daddy either.

"Who's my daddy, then? Is it fat old Uncle Buddy?" I could not keep from crying now.

"Gladys won't tell. I guess, we could ask her again sometime. She might just tell you. If anybody at school or church ever says anything to you, I want you to tell me about it."

I told her I would. "Am I still Heddy and Penny's sister?" I slithered off Mama's lap and pulled my nightgown over my knees, trying to hold myself together.

"You sure are. You're the best sister they could ever have." Mama hugged me tight and kissed me even though my cheeks were wet and snotty. "Just think about what good care you take of those two."

We sat without talking for a while. "Is that why Papa Jim doesn't ask me to his house or give me presents?"

Mama took another big breath. "I guess it probably is, but he ought to be ashamed of himself for it."

Mama always told everybody that I was her prettiest baby and she still calls me her China doll—freckles and all.

"Can I tell Penny?"

"Nicole Marie, this is your story, you tell whoever you want to. Just let it soak in for a while."

"What do I call Aunt Gladys now?"

"I'm your Mama, Nic, nothing has changed."

I must have fallen asleep on the couch because I don't remember going to bed. And the next morning, when I woke up I was in bed with Penny. The first thing I thought of was what Mama had told me the night before. I hoped I'd dreamt it, but knew I hadn't. Even though it was all I thought about, I didn't mention any of what Mama had told me to Penny or anybody for almost a month. It scared me to think that I was different from my sisters. Would they still like me if they knew. All my aunts and uncles and grandparents knew and the only one to treat me any different was Papa Jim. I was so jumbled up and sad inside, I couldn't even come up with questions.

I let the unsettling news settle inside my head. I let it roll around in my brain until it found a comfortable corner. It was Tuesday when I heard a voice inside me say, "Nickle, it's the truth, and it's not ever going to change no matter what." I didn't have any idea what the voice meant—"the truth" could've been about Poppy dying, or Daddy Skinner and Papa Jim being mean, or my "feel sorry," or anything. After days and days of wondering what "the truth" was, I figured it didn't matter because all those things were true and no amount of wishing would ever make them go away, but mostly it didn't matter because the voice had called me "Nickel." Even though I hated it when Poppy called me that, hearing it this time felt soothing, like Poppy was watching after me.

It wasn't until the Saturday between Christmas and New Year's that Mama got that far off look in her eyes again. We'd finished supper and were playing crazy eights on the green-flowered living room rug. Mama was stretched out on the couch, singing to Heddy in a baby blue voice when Penny and I climbed up too. We cuddled in on either side of her. Mama started to fiddle with a curl on my forehead when her song came to the end. "That was pretty, Mama," Heddy said, clapping her hands like a shiny baby seal.

I spied around Mama and Heddy at Penny. She looked at me and shook her head to mean "yes," knowing why I was looking at her. I leaned into Mama's side as close as I could get. I listened to the contented sounds of Heddy sucking her thumb and to the sighs of Penny trying hard not to.

"Tell my story, Mama, my 'feel sorry,' please, please. Penny and Heddy want to hear it too."

THE SCENT OF SASSAFRAS

Louis was already forty-eight years old when he touched down in our midst. Before that, his life had consisted entirely of work, church, the war and its remnants, maintaining the chalk, matte finish on his '53 Dodge pick-up, and little else, unless you count the occasional date with one of Gray Hampton's few unmarried women.

Why, after all those years of bachelorhood, he decided to marry my mom, Sal Barkley, was a mystery to all who knew him. He had to have heard "the talk" about her fiery temper, not to mention the fact that having been widowed six years earlier, she'd been left with three daughters to raise. There was even talk of that temper of hers contributing in some manner to her widowhood.

But, on a frigid February morning in 1955, Louis married her anyway. Penny was ten and Nicole twelve at the time—not particularly the best ages for girls to welcome a new man into their lives. Nicole took every opening to tell him, "You are not my daddy."

I'm Heddy, and I was five and a half at the time of the nuptials.

I hadn't spent much time around men; and after the honeymoon, when Louis moved in—not just into our house, but into the bedroom I had shared my whole life with my mother, I speculated warily as to what else I might lose—my preferred place at the supper table by the window, my station between Mom and Penny in the pew; who knew? Penny and Nicole, who had been in a semi-constant state of feuding prior to the wedding, now huddled up, conspiring ways to sabotage him—salting his coffee, breaking his cigarettes in half, and adding a hint of starch to the laundry when washing his underwear. I did not participate in their collusions, nor did they ask me to.

Lucky for him, I was completely in awe of the oodles of tools, chests, hooks, ramps, creepers, and assorted liquids for powering, cleaning, and quieting engines that he had brought to this union; none of which could possibly fit inside mom's orderly female domicile.

In order to accommodate this influx of stuff, additional storage would be needed. So, by the spring of 1956, Mom and Louis had made up their minds to build a two-bay garage in the backyard of our white clapboard house on Magnolia Street. One side would be slated for sheltering her green Ford and the other for parking his two-toned pick-up, as well as for storing his trove of tools.

The project got rolling with the arrival of a gargantuan yellow bulldozer with the name Euclid inscribed on its side. The operator drove the growling mammoth onto the premises where it began devouring the low hill at the end of the driveway, carving the footprint for a foundation. Penny, Nicole, and I watched the dozer heap its leftovers to the sides and back of the growing cavity, creating a mound that would eventually bound the garage on three sides.

When the driver motioned for me to join him on the seat of the overgrown tractor, I jumped at the chance. I looked around to make sure mom wasn't there to stop me as Louis boosted me up. I waved at my sisters and Louis from my perch. I sat straight and tall like I was on a throne or the back of an elephant. Penny had gotten her camera from the house; she aimed the Brownie at me, taking a snapshot of this momentous event; capturing my entry to arcadia.

I breathed the scent of the red clay and exposed sassafras roots deep into my chest; I scanned the sky to find the sun, and took my own mental snapshots of the surroundings and of Louis's face to remember that day forever.

So, I thought, *this is what it's like to have a dad.*

Mom and Louis both took off work the week of spring break to be with us and to begin construction on the garage. First thing Monday morning, I joined Nicole and Penny at the picnic table—lined up like birds on a wire—waiting for the blossoming to begin. We watched for hours as Louis poured a narrow concrete foundation along all four sides of Euclid's rectangle. We repeated this vigil two days later as Louis began to stack row upon row of concrete blocks.

Mom watched with us, sipping her coffee. Even on her days off, her coffee cup was rimmed with the flagrance of her cardinal red lipstick. We asked her why Louis staggered the blocks instead of stacking one on top of the other. "It makes the wall stronger that way," she said. Then, when Louis waved his newly adopted daughters over and handed each of us a triangular tool, my mother opened her mouth to put a stop to what she thought could only end badly, but went inside instead. Even Nicole grabbed a trowel.

"Just like icing a cake," Louis instructed.

Penny and Nicole lasted about fifteen minutes before deciding to join mom indoors. They still hadn't decided if Louis suited them or not. Penny said he wasn't anything like Poppy, our real dad. My sisters said that when Louis adopted us he had stolen our last connection with Poppy. We were no longer Barkleys, our names were changed to Louis's last name—Craycroft. The changing of our names was a big deal at school, with each of our teachers announcing it to the whole class. They assumed we were all happy about it. I was fine with it, even though I often forgot and stated my name as Heddy Barkley.

Louis laid ten blocks to my one.

When the time came to put the shingles on the roof, Louis climbed up the wooden ladder, and I followed wearing a nail apron tied twice around my waist. I scooted to the place he was working and began dispensing roofing nails three at a time—two for his mouth and one for the hammer.

"Sit still a minute," Louis said. Then he edged behind me and nailed an eight-foot two-by-four to the roof.

"Shove your feet against that plank." He pointed his hammer toward the wooden slat. "That way you won't slide."

I snugged my PF-Flyers tight to the board.

The only time I slipped was when mom shrieked out the window in a voice every bit as earsplitting as the twelve-o'clock whistle.

"For crying out loud," she yelled. "Get Heddy off that roof before you kill her."

I found the window that framed mom's frantic face.

"Heddy's fine. I made sure of it," Louis said.

I shifted my eyes between them as they argued over my safety. Until Louis came along, I'd obeyed mom's wishes almost faster than she could get them out of her mouth.

"I won't be able to get a thing done until she's off that roof. Now get her down."

All he said was, "I won't let her fall."

I looked back at the window and she was gone. Every few minutes I'd check to see if the expression on his face had changed—to see if tolerance had turned to tedium.

Besides my grandmother, Mam, Louis was the only other adult I'd ever known who seemed to enjoy the company of a kid. It made me wonder about Ivan Barkley, the poppy I'd never known. Would he have taken pleasure in my company the way Mam and Louis seemed to? My mother and my sisters had often lamented his passing and expressed sadness over my never having laid eyes on him. I tried to make myself feel sad about it too. I thought it might prove a useful exoneration sometime should I find myself in hot water. But,

I couldn't seem to muster any sorrow over it.

Mom says that before Ivan died, without even knowing I was on the way, he told her if they ever had another daughter he'd like for her to be named Heddy—after his grandmother. I can live with the name "Heddy," and I'm very happy they did not opt for the grandmother's full given name of Hedwig—a name that sounds like an irritating bug that has taken up residence in a person's ear or some misspelled hairpiece.

After we finished the roof, I helped Louis putty-in wavy glass panes for windows, and when the local quarry dumped three loads of gravel, it took all of us to rake it into the garage and all over the driveway. But the high point of this scheme came when Louis attached a basketball hoop to the peak of the garage roof. I figured he had meant it as a surprise since he pulled the rusted iron halo and half-moon of plywood from beneath a tarp in the bed of his truck like he'd been hiding it.

When mom saw the "surprise," she pursed her lips in a way that usually meant she was displeased. "I don't recall our discussing this," she said. "I won't have you turning all three of these girls into tomboys." She cocked her eyes toward me. "Besides, you can't bounce a ball on this gravel." Hearing neither agreeance nor argument, she flattened her palms to the small of her spine, leaned her head back, and examined the perfect blue sky. It seemed to me at the time that she was getting the idea that the rhythm of her ironing, sweeping, and breathing would soon beat to the crunch and clunks of dribbles and shots.

Not a month after the rim had been mounted I was awakened in the middle of the night by the sound of *boing scrunch, boing scrunch scrunch*, that was followed with hushed laughter and words I could barely make out. I pulled back the sheer curtain next to my bed and saw my mother aiming the basketball at the goal and Louis standing next to her, demonstrating the required arm and leg movements for shooting a free throw.

"Bend your knees," he said as he poked at the back of her legs. "Now cradle the ball in front of you with your left hand and push it toward the basket with the other."

It was early Saturday morning and they'd been to a dance the night before at St. George's Knights of Columbus hall.

Boing scrunch. "I can't hit that dang hole," she said as she stumbled slightly backwards, giggling. I thought about waking my sisters as I watched mom and Louis doubled over in laughter. I sat back on my heels half pleased, half jealous, but completely astonished at seeing her seeming to have a good time.

"I don't think you'll make the team," Louis said. Sal slapped at him in mock anger, and he put his arm around her waist and led her toward the house. It was a scene as foreign and unfamiliar as the ocean and palm trees on Gladys's picture postcards from California.

□

Now with the garage finished and crowned by the hoop and backboard, it didn't take long for the locals to chance dropping by with overheated motors and faltering engines. Maybe they saw Louis loitering outside more evenings than before or maybe they just mistook the garage's purpose. Whatever the reason, Gray Hamptoners began showing up with their mowers, cars, and pick-ups for Louis to fix. And much to my mother's miff over the resulting clutter and mess, fix them he did—though only after having worked all day in another man's garage. Since leaving the army, where he'd learned his trade as a Jeep and tank mechanic, Louis had spent the intervening twenty-four years working, repairing, and maintaining cars and trucks at Cooper Motors.

It didn't take a genius to realize that Louis was in his element when in communion with a motor. Even though he seldom had much to say, I could tell he was happy by the way he hummed, whistled, or manipulated his toothpick while he worked. His face and eyes looked calmer and steadier when he was gazing into the maw of an engine. It was an intense focus that made it seem like he could smell or hear or sense the cause of the trouble before he could actually see it. My hunch was confirmed on a sunny Saturday in 1960 when Daniel Vertrees showed up with his '53 Mercury. I thought Louis was practically a magician the way he instantly uncovered the difficulty.

"It doesn't want to start up in the mornings," Daniel Vertrees explained, leaning his head out the car window. "Won't turn over for almost five minutes, just keeps grinding." He ran his finger in circles to indicate the repetition. "Think you can fix it?"

"Cut the engine," Louis said, and he charmed open the Merc's hood like a cobra emerging from its basket, exposing its deceitful, counterfeit eyes. When Daniel Vertrees tried to start it again, Louis leaned his head in close and listened to the *errr erring* for a while then touched a wand-like screwdriver to some mysterious spot deep in the motor. "Try her now," he said. The troubled vehicle started right up.

Louis wiped his hands and the screwdriver with a clean rag. "Probably the solenoid," he said. "You'll need a new one."

I had seen Louis install these coils of wire, and he'd explained how the solenoid had to do with magnets and electricity and getting current to the starter. But even after watching him secure it in place with pins and bolts, and connecting the wires to ones deep inside the motor, I still didn't understand its workings. The beauty for me was not the precision of the engine or the smooth hum of a motor with all its cylinders snapping in perfect timing, it was the precision and hum of Louis making it all flow like 10w30 motor oil.

I was shooting baskets a day or two later when Daniel Vertrees again waddled down our driveway. He tucked his cigarette between his lips and pouched his hands in front of his bushel-basket belly. I passed him the ball. He took one step closer to the hoop and fired up a lead-footed jump shot, then two more. "Is she ready?" he asked Louis in a breathless wheeze, this time sinking his attempt.

Louis nodded, lit a Tareyton, and used it to point to the Merc's wheels. "You've only got about another thousand miles on those tires," he said. "Cooper's putting their Goodyear's half price on Saturday."

Daniel Vertrees bounce-passed the basketball to me and stepped away from the imaginary foul line. "Thanks," he said, resting his palms on his knees and sucking in big gulps of air. Finally, he caught his breath enough to trawl a twenty out of his wallet.

"That oughtta cover it." Louis stuffed the crisp bill in his shirt pocket next to his pencil and tire pressure gauge.

I hoped mom wasn't watching because I knew she'd complain for half an hour about how little Mr. Vertrees had paid for the work. She always twisted her mouth into a sour look whenever she saw Louis accept whatever payment the customer offered. One day, to appease her, Louis agreed to draw up a menu of prices for the different services he provided to display or furnish folks with when they showed up. Mom even went to the trouble of typing and mimeographing copies for him. But the sheets wound up under a bevy of tools and used motor parts and never in the grip of a single patron. Mom was too neat and organized to appreciate the beauty and creativity of Louis's ways. But she finally gave up, especially, once Louis tendered the wad of cash he pocketed each week.

Mom never stayed around the garage long enough to see that there was perfection and proportion in Louis's seeming disarray. If you observed him regularly, as I did, a pattern as natural and intuitive as Euclid's golden ratio would begin to emerge; as a rag was never more than an arm's length away, the tools used most often were alternately splayed and spiraled atop the workbench, and the cost of the service provided always precisely paralleled that of the payment offered. Over the months and years, I became as familiar with the layout and location of the garage's paraphernalia as Louis, and could even offer a bit of assistance.

If Louis said, "Hand me a three-quarter," I could pick the wrench out of the red Craftsman drawer and slap it in his palm as crisply as the nurses on the Dr. Kildare Show handed the surgeon his scalpels. And on top of learning to tell if the stain on the driveway was caused by a transmission leak or an oil leak, I learned that it was okay to be on the quiet side—even if mom did call me bashful. After all, Louis was quiet and he seemed to get along in the world.

Though I couldn't have spoken it then, at age ten or eleven, I'd already suspected that of all the tools in Louis's chest, the most valuable was his peaceful heart. I knew this the same way I had sensed that the one-true-religion doctrine taught by the well-intentioned and pious nuns at St. George's was not exactly the gospel truth; that neither the pagan babies for whom we were urged to pray, nor my Baptist cousins, could possibly be sentenced to purgatory or damned to hell just for not being Catholic like me. When I mentioned my theory to Louis, he said he thought I might be right, but that it would be best if I kept it to myself.

Louis and I passed countless hours wordlessly puttering and pondering in our temple of tools. But then came the times when the quiet hum of activity would be replaced by snores and rumbles when Louis had, once again, fallen asleep. Ever since he'd come to live with us, I had noticed that he was prone to spontaneous napping, but it was sometime after my tenth birthday that I realized his catnaps had begun to increase.

I'd find him dead asleep, lying half under a Ford on Lazy Louie—the rolling board Louis used to scoot himself under cars—or nodding his head at the breakfast table with his hand still wrapped around his coffee cup. When I'd come upon him in this state, I'd drop a spoon in the sink, or a wrench on the ground, or I'd taunt our dog, Freckles, into barking. Louis would then break into a whistle or a sputter to let me know he'd come to, or try and make me think he hadn't been sleeping at all.

Neither downpours, July's steamy heat, nor Louis's impromptu naps could keep me away from the garage. A musty place already, the rain and humidity intensified the smells and gave the air a slippery texture that slickened the garage's trappings along with my own hair and hide. This atmosphere led to sleepy afternoons and evenings that seemed to stretch farther than the clock truly measured.

Only a dire need to use the bathroom would press either of us to venture indoors. But on each one's return, a fresh refill of tea would be smuggled out. Were the day stormy and windy, we would often have to scoot our chairs a few feet deeper into our sanctuary to stay dry.

One particularly gray and drizzly Sunday afternoon in '61, I had slipped indoors to refill our glasses when I heard my mother, Penny, and Nicole talking in the sewing room.

"It's a shame she's not a boy," Penny said over the whirr of the Singer.

"I know what you mean," Mom replied. "He'd worship the very ground a boy walked on."

I squatted on my haunches to listen.

"She acts nearly like a boy now," Nicole said. "Never washes her hair and smells like some pint-sized grease monkey." All three of them started to laugh and I pulled a piece of hair under my nose like a mustache.

Here all along I'd thought Louis was okay with me the way I was. A twinge of something I didn't understand pinched at my chest and made me want to cry. I thought about creeping into my mother's bedroom and hiding her favorite cameo earrings like I'd done when she hadn't let me keep Goldie. Mam had told me I could have the yellow kitten if it was okay with my mother. Mom never missed the cameo clip-ons, because I returned them to their rightful place the next day. But, for just a little while, it had made me feel satisfied and in control to be the only one who'd known where her prized jewelry had been hidden. I wanted to feel that way now. But instead of stealing again, I slipped back outside to the solace of the garage and Louis.

"Where's our drinks?" He asked. I slouched in my chair not answering and stared in the direction of the rain. Freckles jumped in my lap and Louis returned to the mower blade he was sharpening. I pulled my hair up on top of my head and slapped on the Cincinnati Reds baseball cap I kept in the garage, the same one that mom had threatened to burn if she saw me wearing it again. I pulled the hem of my faded, over-sized T-shirt to my face and wiped my runny nose.

As Louis was honing the mower's blade to a knife-edge, I blurted out over the harsh scrape of the grinder, "Bet you wish you'd married somebody who had a boy instead of all these dumb girls?"

Louis slowly straightened his bent frame and unplugged the grinder. He sauntered over and sat his chair next to mine. I couldn't see his face, but I knew his eyes would look tender. He picked up a rag and wiped the grass stains off his hands. Those hands of his that could fix just about anything always got my attention. Grime was permanently imbedded in his fingerprints and his palms were calloused and rough. He regularly trimmed his fingernails, but not short like most men's, he left enough nail to assist with picking up slender gaskets and pins that often fell through a motor to the ground.

Then, in a voice as quiet as the rain I said: "Mom and them say you wish I was a boy. I heard them talking when I went in. Said you'd worship the very ground a boy walked on." I bit back tears, not wanting to seem like a crybaby. I was content spending time with Louis and it just about killed me to think that mom and my sisters might be right.

Louis took a long drag on his cigarette, brushed silvery dust off his shirt. He exhaled smoke into the clammy air. "You want me to worship you?" he asked, angling his head toward me.

"Noooo," I said, meaning "yes."

"To tell you the truth, I haven't had the first thought about it.

Boy, girl—doesn't seem to matter much to me. We do all right, don't we, Squirt?" He snapped his rag at my chair.

I looked at his rugged and grooved face and thought about how he had never given any indication that I might come up lacking in the gender department or in any other area for that matter. I smiled at him and grabbed at the rag. "I guess so," and Louis returned to grinding the blade. I lifted that hat just enough to release my hair back down my spine.

It must have rained or stormed everyday that week, leaving the ground littered with twigs and leaves. By Saturday the weather had cleared, and the air had cooled off a little. When I came outside that morning, I was surprised to see that all the cars and mowers had been picked up by their owners. The only vehicles around were Louis's truck and Mom's new blue Ford Falcon.

"Let's clean this place up," Louis said, leaning against the garage doorframe with his arms folded.

He let me back the car and the truck onto the driveway to empty both bays. I lined up two chairs while Louis filled a Maxwell House coffee can with carburetor cleaner. He sat the can on the ground between the chairs and laid a couple work rags over its lip. I gathered the crescents, pliers, and ratchets that littered the surface of the spongy, grease-coated workbench. The wrenches were encrusted with a grainy black muck that made the fractions engraved on their necks indecipherable. I dumped as many tools into the cleaner as the can would hold. I turned on the radio and Louis seated a toothpick between his teeth, as that always seemed to help him put off smoking.

We each pulled a single shank out of the fluid and scrubbed to the beat of Hank William's *Jambalaya.*

Goodbye Joe, we gotta go,
Me Oh, My Oh

"Why doesn't the tea spill over my glass when the ice melts," I asked, wiping at the jaws of a pair of pliers and watching my glass sweat in the languid August humidity.

"Fills up the same place as the cubes." He grabbed another tool.

I took a swig of my drink and stared at the glass. I felt like I was seeing it for the first time. I considered his answer, which seemed to make such perfect sense, and wondered why I hadn't figured it out myself. I sat the glass in front of me and watched the cubes turn to water. I pulled out another wrench.

"What does it feel like to have a heart attack?" I asked, recalling an uncle's recent mild coronary.

"Like a ton of bricks, right in the ticker." He gazed at his grime-free wrench as if he could see his reflection in it.

"What are you thinking about, Daddy?"

"Not much—maybe, about how good these tools'll look when we get finished."

"What else?"

"I'm thinking there's just enough yard mess from the storm to make a decent fire."

Son of gun, we'll have big fun
On the bayou

The soaking and wiping and re-stowing took us until after three-thirty. And when I saw Louis grab a rake, I knew he was fixing to build the fire.

I ran in the house and yelled to my mother and sisters, "Daddy's raking up sticks for a fire. Want to have a roast?"

"This is sure to ruin our supper—eating at four o'clock." Mom lowered her skewered marshmallows and hot dog into the blaze. "But it's a heck of a fine way to do it." Her normal scowl had softened into a look as mellow as that of cat just awakened from its nap. What more could she ask for, I thought—a simple supper, no dishes to wash, no cars cluttering her driveway, and a clean garage.

As I stuffed three gooey white orbs in my mouth, I noticed mom looking at my hands that were every bit as grimy as Louis's. Wrinkles deepened around her mouth and between her eyebrows, but she kept eating. It seemed like she might have finally accepted the fact that dirt was not lethal. If it was, her second husband would certainly be as dead as her first by now.

The five of us sat around the fireplace full-belly satisfied until the only things left were embers and crickets. Mom, Penny, and Nicole tossed their paper plates into what was left of the fire and returned to the house to finish their Saturday routine cleaning, sewing, baking, and ironing before *Dick Clark* and *Perry Mason* came on television.

While Louis shoveled the ashes into a five-gallon bucket to cool, I scooped up the towels he'd placed in a pile for washing, the rags we used over and over to wipe our hands, tools, car parts, spills, and spits. It was most likely these rags that were the carriers of the "garage smell" my mother and sisters liked to complain about.

After dumping the rags into the washer, I returned and found Louis sitting on a nail keg against a wall inside his orderly garage. He'd re-parked the car and truck in the bays and must have sat down to rest. As I got closer, I noticed his hands in his lap, they were barely holding on to his open billfold. Then the evenness of his breath and sagging head and shoulders, told me he'd drifted off again. I looked at his pants and shirt, and like all his work clothes, they were vented with cigarette burns from all the times he'd fallen asleep while smoking.

I figured he had been checking to see if he had enough cash for tomorrow morning's collection plate when he dozed off. I started singing along with the radio in a voice as loud as I could manage.

But sleep won't come,
The whole night through.
Your Cheatin Heart will tell on you

"You think old Freck needs a bath while we're at it?" Louis asked, clearing his throat and stuffing his wallet back in his hip pocket. I groaned, thinking I should've let him sleep, and began filling the metal washtub for the ensuing dog wash. I wouldn't hear of or read about the condition called *narcolepsy* until much later, when I was in college.

Not two months later that fall, I ran inside the house, slamming the door in an effort to awaken him in the likelihood that he was asleep. I had raced ahead of my mother to make sure he hadn't burnt another hole in the rug, scorched the tabletop with his cigarette, or left a pot of coffee to boil dry on the stove. Earlier in the day, I had ridden with mom to take Nicole and Penny back to boarding school after a weekend visit at home. She insisted that they go to the expensive school even though she could scarcely afford it. It was where the "best" families at St. George's sent their girls for high school, including our Barkley cousins and the Coopers.

When I got to the living room, the World Series was playing on TV and a gray/white smoke cloud swarmed up from the chair Louis was sitting in.

"Wake up, Daddy," I screamed, picking up his glass and tossing lukewarm tea in his lap. Louis jumped out of the chair, exposing a four-inch fissure seared into the pink flowered cushion, its edges were brown and ragged, and the beige cottony stuffing inside it smoldered and reeked.

"Did you get burned?" I set the glass back on the coaster and folded my arms across my chest, trying to hold back the churning terror.

He examined the thighs of his coveralls, "Only a little singed." He hurried to the kitchen to get a towel.

I was fanning the smoke when my mother walked in.

"What's that smell?" she asked. "What've you done?"

Louis showed Sal the damage. He apologized and promised, "I'll get you a new one," referring to the disfigured chair.

Mom's mouth fell open. "You could've burnt down the house! Killed yourself!" She left unspoken her fear of being widowed for a second time, but we both knew it was what she had immediately thought. Her eyes were fierce and angry in their glare. Her arm reached out and I gasped, thinking she was about to slap Louis's face. Instead she snatched the cushion off the chair and disappeared in the direction of the sewing room. I put my hands over my ears to muffle the house-jarring door slam I knew would follow.

"Guess I deserved that." Louis frowned as he collected his ashtray and glass and turned off the Reds and the Yankees and he ambled out of the room and away from the newest evidence of his affliction.

He sat down at the kitchen table where I was making baloney and Miracle Whip sandwiches. We ate silently, focused on our plates and our concerns. I wished that Penny and Nicole were around to soothe mom's frazzled nerves, as it was something I had never been able to do. They would've accompanied her into the sewing room and spoken in quick, hushed and blaming tones about the way it could have been, the way it should have been. But I imagine that Sal Skinner Barkley Craycroft knew full well the potential damaging result that can come with too much blaming.

Louis stuffed a Lay's potato chip in his mouth and said, "I could use your help changing the wheels on Nelson's mower when we're done eating." He said it as calmly as though the events of the last hour had amounted to dripping a spot of tea onto the chair, then he bit into another chip.

I pulled the entire rim of crust off my bread and was molding it into letters and shapes on the Formica surface. "I sort of wish you'd quit smoking," I said, intent on the shapes I'd drawn.

He downed the last of his tea and fished a toothpick out of his shirt pocket. "Did you happen to catch who won that ballgame?"

Having gotten the answer I'd fully expected, I stood to clear the table to hide my sniffing and tears.

"I think the Reds were up. I'll be out after I wash the dishes."

When I ventured out to the garage, I saw a man I didn't recognize standing with one foot on the bumper of Louis's Dodge. He gestured toward an ancient brown and white saddle-oxford of a Chevrolet that was as rusty and hump-backed as Mam.

"She hasn't got a ounce of pep," the man was saying. "And she cuts out when I push on the gas to go up a hill." I watched Louis raise the hood of the ailing metal geezer and work his magic by merely tightening down the spark plugs.

"Give her a try," Louis said. The man started the old girl. "Now, gun it." Then Louis advised the man to drive around town a couple times, making sure he took the hill on Main Street because if it was going to cut out, it would certainly do so while climbing that hill.

Within fifteen minutes the stranger was steering the vintage auto between the two overgrown yews on either side of the driveway. He was grinning so big you'd have thought he was driving a brand new Cadillac. I had to stifle my own grin as the man shoved a handful of bills into Louis's palm. I hoped mom was watching this time.

After the man left, I climbed onto the roof of the Dodge truck's cab, resting my legs on the windshield. Daddy squatted as effortlessly as Yogi Berra on the garage floor, changing the wheels on Nelson's lawnmower. He could sit that way for an hour or more—flat footed—Chinese.

There was a cork board nailed above the workbench; and pinned to it were spare keys and notes and even a faded copy of the price list my mother had typed years before. Next to it was that snapshot of me sitting on Euclid when I was just five years old.

In the rick-rack-edged photo, I was sitting aloft and gazing down at Louis—much like now. Those hands of his were resting on his hips and his head was arced back looking up at me on the seat of the dozer. Atop the truck, I closed my eyes and inhaled the root-beer scent of sassafras and the cool dampness of freshly turned red clay. I could feel the sun's warming rays even though the sun had already dissolved below the horizon. For the moment I was back to 1955—innocent and protected.

My eyes resisted opening as my mind wanted to stay where it was, but a familiar rasp beckoned me out of my fantasy. I slid on my rear down the windshield to the hood and kept sliding until my shoes caught the bumper. It was an easy skip to the ground where, still in his baseball catcher's squat, his snoring wheezed full-mouthed. I stared at the burning cigarette that had fallen from his yellow-stained fingers. Out of habit, my foot slid toward it to crush it, but halted mid-step. I bent down and tweezed my thumb and index finger on either side of the half-gone butt and raised it to my lips. I smoked it all the way to the filter, and then ground it out with my toe. It wasn't my first time to sneak a puff, nor would it be my last. Rebellion had begun its reign, trumping even Louis and the garage. In the mind of a twelve-year-old, the double duties of keeping Louis safe and maintaining peace in the family loomed as ominous as storm clouds amassed in every corner of the sky. The haven that once provided shelter had warped from temple to tempest.

I pilfered three Tareytons from the pack Louis had left on the workbench and hid them in my pocket. As I was leaving Louis and the garage, I paused and reversed my steps. I clamored through a drawer of wrenches where my fingers let a ½ inch crescent teeter and tumble, then clatter and rattle and clang.

YORKIE MILLS'S HINDRANCE

As if this day could get any worse, the hindrance had shown up again. It was clinging to the screen door of her paint-starved shack, warming itself in the morning sun. Her daddy had left her the house nearly fifty years ago and she never found a reason to leave it or the worn-out mining camp in which it'd been built. Yorkie has wrung out a living here, taking in washing, ironing, and mending for women in the town. Her only companions have been the hindrance and the occasional troubled girl who'd sought her out.

"Damn you!" Yorkie swore at the screen door and staggered as her clothesbasket slipped from her hands and slapped the linoleum floor. She had never understood why that snake wanted to torment her, showing up like it was God's gift. She stood there a moment, rubbing her chest as if that might calm her thumping heart.

Yorkie bent down and collected her spilt laundry, packing each piece back into the fraying wicker basket. She used her foot to scoot it out of the June sun that blazed through the door. She welcomed the rays that splashed both rooms this time of the morning with their white, clarifying light shining right through the glass pickle jar that harbored and purified her cherished tools. This was the only time of day that she was reminded of the mint green shade the walls had once flaunted. She had yet to come up with a name for the dreary hue that entombed her for the remaining hours.

The house still smelled of bacon, eggs, and coffee now shriveling on an unwashed plate and cup. Nowadays she only washed dishes once a day—after supper, when she had dirtied the last.

Yorkie glanced at the mending on top of the sewing machine. But instead of taking up her needles, she eased her barking bones into the rocking chair that resided in the kitchen corner, where she could study the curve of the black snake that clutched her screen, and where she could bide away time until the hindrance moved along.

She used her hand to wipe the dust off the top of the radio that sat beside her. The thing needed to be put in the closet, since it had never worked, but Yorkie loved the look of it on her side table. One of the women she sewed and washed for had given it to her last Christmas. She'd wished for one all fall and winter so she could listen to President Kennedy's inauguration ceremony. Even though she'd had it for months, she had yet to get a human sound out of it; certainly nothing that sounded like an inauguration, no matter how she twisted the knobs. She did not keep up with politics, but still she was excited about the election of John Fitzgerald Kennedy; though she wondered what he would think of her, him being a member of the Catholic faith, and them with all their condemnation of any sort of birth control. But Yorkie liked him anyway and thought he and his brother would do a fine job with their Harvard degrees and legal know-how. Thinking about what lay ahead of them made Yorkie tired.

This was the first time she had rested since breakfast; her first chance to smell the honeysuckle that bloomed in the garden outside her window or to tie up the boots she'd slid her feet inside at dawn. She pulled her long graying hair to one side and braided it into a rope that fell at least half a yard down her back, mimicking her spine. She pulled out her pen and crinkled pad to review and revise the sermon, speech, pep talk that she gave to the girls who came to her. She had authored the treatise when she was in her twenties and continued to modify it, trying to make it say what she wanted it to. Her intent was to take away or, at the very least, to ease their disgrace and their guilt; what she knew from experience they were going through.

The gist of the talk was that she didn't want a single girl to leave her house feeling ashamed—not of what had brought them there, not of laying-up with a boy, and not of getting shed of the problem; a daunting task to say the least. She thought it was one thing to learn from an experience and to feel remorse over it, but shame killed a person's spirit; rotted their soul. So she wrote and re-wrote her speech often and even practiced it out loud to make sure she got it right. The hindrance had listened to the talk so many times that if he'd been a verbal creature, he could have delivered it himself.

Yorkie knew the speech was as much for her as for the girls; it's what she wished she had heard from her daddy instead of the hateful and spiteful remonstrance he had jabbed into her.

Satisfied for now with the changes, she put down her pen and pad and gave the snake a good hard stare, hoping to detect movement—willing its departure. The serpent could appear and disappear from the door with the bat of an eye. Yorkie might look up from having swatted at a fly and the thing would be gone. Now and again, this gave Yorkie reason to question the soundness of her faculties. "Maybe I should've wished for a camera instead of this no-good radio. I'd shoot your picture for proof."

She wondered if the snake took pleasure in her confinement or in causing her to feel flapdoodle. Was the creature capable of such inclinations? Yorkie knew better. But then the hindrance hadn't been the only one who'd confined her.

The creature reminded her of her own daddy, even though he was long dead and gone—the way it hemmed her in.

Evenings when Yorkie was a girl, her father would position a porch chair in the yard so it faced the door and gave him a clear view of the road at the same time. Yorkie dragged one leg over top of the other, just the way she remembered him sitting in that chair. Then he'd lay his head back with his hat put over his eyes like he was in for a nap. She pictured him with his shotgun across his lap and his arms laced behind his head for a pillow. Anything that moved within earshot, he'd draw a bead in the direction of the noise before Yorkie could so much as look at him. As it turned out, he had reason to worry.

This was the old man's way of running off any young men who came sniffing around the mining camp, and how he kept Yorkie from going off with any of them. She always surmised that this was the reason she was still alone—him never allowing her to go courting. Any callers finally just gave up. All she was left with besides this shack were the skills he'd taught her, a treadle sewing machine, that shotgun, and a trunk of clothes. So, here she remained, washing other people's laundry, helping out girls, and being jailed by a conniving snake.

Yorkie gazed off, seeming to consider that earlier time. She'd gotten over any lingering bitterness, but the loneliness had soaked into her; hollowing her heart and brittling her bones.

Of all the callers, Daniel hung on the longest, too long some would say. Her mind protested when she tried to come up with his last name, even though she never thought she'd forget the sound of it, as she had believed it would one day be hers. But she could still see his face plain as day—pink cheeked from the weather with a dimple dug deep into his chin. His hair shined blacker than the ace of spades—about like the hindrance's hide—but he had eyes as green as the jealous streak that ran up her daddy's spine; and freckles, even on his back. Her father would have killed him if he'd known then that Yorkie was on speaking terms with every one of those dear brown dots. Yorkie grinned at the vision of Daniel in her mind.

Yorkie met Daniel when he came to the camp to collect leftover bits and pieces of cloth, could say rags, from any of the residents who'd give him some. It was how he helped his family get by. He told Yorkie that his mother used the best pieces in quilt tops and the rest to stuff them. He learned it was best to visit Yorkie early in the afternoon before the old man got in from the mine. If Danny stayed too late, he'd climb the maple tree that stood close by and hide until Yorkie and her father sat down to supper, then he'd slip off.

She thought about one time in particular when she and Daniel had been too tangled up to hear her father approaching. But they were abruptly brought-to at the clatter of him cocking his shotgun up next to Danny's temple. They tried sneaking out a few times after that, but Danny'd been spooked. One day, he just quit showing up. She continued going to their regular spot in the woods for a full month, but he never came again.

She looked around at her place and wondered how her life might have been with a husband and a couple of kids. After all, it was Daniel who'd gotten her in trouble. But he was long gone before she even knew she was expecting. It was her daddy who noticed her swelling belly. He brewed up a potion and made her drink it. The elixir was guaranteed to cause her to expel the infant, and certainly the beating she'd gotten would ensure it. She drank the concoction several times a day for a week. When it had no effect, he took things into his own hands. He had not used a coat hanger, but whatever it was caused her to pass out from the pain. She knew he had fine instruments to use and she'd never heard any of the other girls scream in pain the way she had. The only conclusion she could draw was that he'd wanted her to hurt; he'd wanted her to pay for her wrongdoings.

She'd wondered it before, but now even more—had her mother gotten herself in trouble like Yorkie? Had she come to her daddy, James Mills for help? Of course, she'd never know, but it did give her pause.

She was twelve years old when her daddy enlisted her assistance with the medical procedures. Before this she hadn't understood why so many young girls and women came to see him in the evenings. She saw him give them the herbs and instructions and they would pay him money. Some returned for the medical procedure, but not many. Those who returned had to pay more money, which seemed, somehow, wrong to Yorkie. The old man ranted on and on to the girls and anyone who might have accompanied them about reading their Bibles and how they should be ashamed of their offenses. But, his remedial technique was gentle and evidently painless and not one cried out, and not one returned because of infection or related illness. Yorkie had to admit that he'd taught her well.

Yorkie brushed a gnat out of her face like she was trying to brush her thoughts away.

"Not much use in thinking about that now," she said, watching her tormentor, and wishing she could summon the gumption to take the broom to the door. She had done it once before, and the snake did scurry off. But her act of bravery ended up backfiring on her, as the clever creature wiggled itself right inside the holes in her brand new steps.

Last fall when her wood stoop rotted off, Yorkie paid Frankie Sue, a child living across the camp, five dollars to build new steps so she could get in and out the door easy.

Yorkie was certain the child's mama had marked it by giving it that name. She was all the time having to say "that child" or call it by its full name, as nobody knew whether to say "he or she." The child must have been close to thirteen and every soul in camp was watching for something to bud. The sweet child wore a clean set of overalls everyday that hid any hint to its gender and kept its hair short enough to keep everybody guessing.

Yorkie's own plight wasn't much different than Frankie Sue's. After all her housedresses wore out, she dug into that trunk her daddy left her. She rolled up his shirtsleeves, cut the britches off where they'd be right, and cinched his belt up tight around her waist, and went on. Taking in washing and mending didn't bring in enough to buy piece goods for dresses. She had managed to hold on to one good dress; one that had once belonged to her mother, but she saved it for funerals and for when the troubled girls came to her. It was long and gray, the same somber pigment as her braid; but it made her feel elegant and capable—proficient like a teacher or a nurse. Yorkie was still thin even though she was up in age and she even felt a twinge of pride in being able to fit into the dress her mother had worn at the age of nineteen.

Frankie Sue stacked up a slew of concrete blocks laid on their sides to give Yorkie three steps, three blocks across from the door to the ground. Yorkie asked, "Child, now what are you going to do with these dollars you just earned making me this fine set of steps?" She had hoped the child would say to buy herself a dress or to buy himself a fishing pole, but the child smiled a Kool-Aid grin and said, "I'm going to buy me a new set of overalls," and ran back across camp. Still so skinny this summer, they're all confounded yet.

The snake's tongue hissed out its mouth a couple times almost as though it had read her thoughts and was laughing at her story. Yorkie laughed too.

She leaned forward in her chair, resting her forearms on her thighs, squinting her eyes and tightening her lips like she was trying to look mean. It was a painful thing for her to admit, but Yorkie had actually given the meddlesome reptile a name. She had never said the name out loud. Yorkie refused to allow herself such foolishness. It was bad enough that she was sitting there with the Bible close enough to lay a hand on, glaring at the devil himself.

Her chest heaved as she remembered a day last week when she was cleaning sticks up out of the yard—after a storm had kept the hindrance hidden all morning; once the sun broke through, she spied the snake slipping out from under her house, sidling its entire length over to a steaming rock by the shed where it curled itself round and around, and raised its head up proud with its black skin shining just like silk. Yorkie was awed by its beauty and got such a swelled-up feeling in her chest that she wondered right then if the hindrance might not just be God. But she quickly reminded herself that the good Lord would never torment a gray-haired woman like this one does. In the Bible, it says we're to love all God's creatures, but Yorkie could not believe this applied to snakes.

All these notions and worries had made Yorkie thirsty, so she strolled to the sink and downed a glass of water, and then drifted back to the rocker. She sat down with a plop and reminded herself to stuff more padding in the seat of the worn-down chair cushion. She figured she could use the old under-britches she had sent to the ragbag, ones long past repairing, to soften it up some. The thought of her ragbag put her back in mind of young Daniel.

She laughed, recalling a warm afternoon when she and Daniel had been chasing each other from ash to pine in the woods, when she landed with her back against a tall oak to catch her breath. All of a sudden, Danny stopped dead still, eyes big as quarters, and said to her, "Don't move Yorkie, don't even breathe if you can help it." He sneaked a stick up off the ground and quick as you could say Danny Tucker, he'd flung the biggest black snake she'd ever seen, twenty feet in the air—probably some kin to the hindrance. It was all she could do to keep from telling her father that night about how Mister Daniel Tucker had saved his only child's life. Thinking about the beating she would have suffered if she had told him still had the power to knock all the joy right out of her.

"Tucker! That's it!" she said, hoping to clear her mind of more unpleasant remembrances. She knew the name would come to her sooner or later. Land sakes, "Yorkie Tucker" doesn't have quite the same ring to it today as it did back then. She had thought it was the finest name she'd ever heard, and even picked out names for their children to go along with it–James, after Yorkie's daddy and Eleanor, after his mama.

When she was born, her daddy named her Jamesina York Mills;

"Jamesina" after himself, and "York" after the state where he claimed to have family. Whenever she asked about her mother, Yorkie's father would answer, "She plainly vanished one Friday before you were a year old; gone when I got in from the mine."

She stood up, fluffed the cushion and hugged it against her chest. Sometimes she thought she could actually remember her mother singing,

Bye-bye baby bunting,
Daddy's gone a hunting,

even though she knew it was completely impossible.

She shook a crooked finger at the snake and sat back down, placing the plumped pillow under her backside. Several minutes passed as she rocked. Yorkie glanced over at the tattered family Bible and remembered a fitting quote: "Now the serpent was more cunning than any beast of the field which the Lord God had made." At this, she bit into one of the cooking apples out of the basket on the table. She shook the half-eaten apple at the door and cackled, "See what you made me do."

She finished her apple and closed her eyes for a moment as if she was praying. Yorkie was grateful for one thing—the snake took care of the mice around her place, making it so she didn't have a bunch of gnawing critters running around her floors all winter. She considered how a cat might serve the purpose just as well, or better; and it being a creature whose name she could say out loud. She saw nothing wrong with folks saying, "That Yorkie Mills might wear man's clothes, but she's got herself one fine mouser," speaking of a fat, handsome tabby—bigheaded staring out her screen door. It seemed far better than folks saying, "That Yorkie Mills spends half her day holed up indoors looking at some snake on her screen door." Her eyes fell shut again, picturing the imaginary feline.

Yorkie stirred in her rocker and figured she must have dropped off. She glared at the nagging clock. "Lord God, the morning has gotten clean away and me without a single sock hung out and a girl maybe coming by this evening. Thank goodness that snake is finally gone."

Yorkie spent many a summer afternoon collecting pennyroyal, blue cohosh, and she could sometimes find coltsfoot, just like her daddy had taught her. Yorkie dried the herbs so she'd have them all winter long. She gave her girls handwritten instructions on when, how much, and how often to drink the potion—just like a doctor. It almost always did the trick. She could count on both hands the times girls had to come for the second time.

Every month one or two girls would seek her out. If it wasn't for Yorkie, it was likely their daddy's would half kill them or, at best, shun or shame them. Yorkie was proud of her skill and thanked the Lord everyday for having given it to her, even though she had learned it the hard way. She would never think of accepting money for her work. Every single girl she'd seen offered her money and Yorkie patted each one on the shoulder and said "Buy something that'll make you feel good about yourself." Then she'd launch into her pep talk. To a girl, not one ever said more than two words back to her, usually, "thanks" or "thank you" was all they could muster.

The only thing she could remember about the girl scheduled for tonight was that she was from Gray Hampton and that she had a funny name, like her own. Yorkie never asked for their last names, but she could remember almost all of her girls' given names. If the girl showed up tonight it would mean that the potion had not been successful.

Yorkie was good at her work. Even one of the women she washed and sewed for had sought her help as a girl, the one who gave her the radio. Now she's a woman married with two children. Yorkie kept her tools clean by boiling them and storing them in an old pickle jar filled with a mixture of alcohol and bleach. She kept a supply of whiskey on hand, but only used it occasionally for other than medicinal purposes.

Yorkie lifted her basket and sheepishly peered out the door. She examined either side of her steps for any sign of the slinking snake. As quick as her legs would take her, she slipped out the door and down the stairs. Once clear of the stoop she slowed and searched the sky for clouds. She sniffed the air, smelling for what she hoped was not rain.

It was odd to think how her screen was vacant all winter long, and her with no reason to venture out the door. Even the wash got hung inside during the cold. She cherished the summer despite the hindrance, and dreaded the time of year when it would stop coming round as that meant the setting-in of another cold and dreary winter. She would see only a few of her girls over the winter, but they were always too scared to talk to her. She never fully understood why they seemed so afraid of her, as she wouldn't hurt a fly or even a snake, much less a woman-child who'd found herself in the same spot that Yorkie had, so many years ago.

While she was pinning the ladies' dresses to the line, Yorkie spied the hindrance lying coiled up on its favorite rock by the shed, shimmering in the sun like it'd just crawled through a puddle of oil. The snake's brilliance distracted Yorkie so powerfully that she pinched her finger with a clothespin. Then without any forewarning, she found herself yearning to touch the scaly black rope; to pick it up and rub it against her coarse cheek. But Yorkie knew better than to do something as harebrained as that. Still, she could feel the snake's eyes watching her, almost like it was measuring the gap between them.

When the socks and slips were hung up, Yorkie stood for a time staring at the snake. And it seemed to Yorkie that the snake was staring back at her. She began to inch her way toward the shed and the sun-drenched creature.

"You watching old Yorkie?" Her trembling legs almost failed her not ten feet from it. The connection of their eyes pulled Yorkie closer, against all reason.

"You better move along. I'm almost to you," she hummed at five feet.

She had always heard that snake's skin was as cold as death even on days as hot as today. "Reckon that's so?" She asked this out loud as though the snake had heard her thought. Yorkie bent her knees as far as they'd go and curved her body forward at the waist in the direction of the snake.

As she reached her fingers toward it, she prayed the Lord's Prayer—as much for the sound as the help. When the tips of her fingers grazed the creature's form, running them faintly across its rings, skimming its scaly hide, Yorkie grew quiet, forgetting the words to her prayer.

She was so shocked at its warmth she drew her hand back. "Why you're not cold at all," she chuckled, "and softer than an old belt's been worn all day."

She gave the snake one last brush with her palm. Then, give out as much from fear as toil, she straightened, arched her back, and turned to go; finally breaking the spell. Behind her, the snake began to uncoil. It slithered across the mossy ground in time with Yorkie's stride, and writhed itself inside the concrete blocks under her feet, just as the lonely old crone lumbered up the stairs and into her house where she would lay out her tools, don her gray dress, and pray that no one arrived.

ONE DEADLY SIN

Here it was only the end of May and already warm enough to coax a chorus of heat bugs into song. Heddy's children, Ben (twelve) and Lilly (almost nine) always delighted in their harmonic chant because it usually meant that school was out, or would be soon. In just days, they'd be in and out of the house dozens of times a day with their friends—making Kool-Aid popsicles, poking holes in the lids of jars stuffed with grass, and on rainy days, creating room-sized forts out of blankets and quilts on chairs.

She was still miffed at Ben over him letting his bike get stolen, especially once he'd admitted that it was his tardiness to tennis practice that caused him to leave it unlocked. This morning when he asked her for a ride to practice, she said, "You'll have to find your own way."

Having to say and do this sort of thing is what she hated about parenting—that need to insert a teaching filter over her heart's natural inclinations. It wasn't as though driving him would be difficult for her. But the parenting manual would label her as "enabling irresponsibility" if she gave in. Why did things have to get so complicated?

When Joe told her how he had caught Ben and his friend, Shamus, in the garage igniting aerosol paint spray with a Bic lighter, she realized she was entering new territory, one that would require her to learn many new filtering techniques. Her heart would no longer be enough. All reason out the window.

When Heddy was a girl she'd found her own mother to be over-bearing and interfering; after all, she thought, what could possibly happen to me. Now that she has had her own children, she found the relentless balancing act arduous and exhausting—weighing every word, questioning every action—hers and Joe's, as well as Ben's and Lilly's. Will it be like this forever, she wondered?

She gazed out her kitchen window, admiring the forest that bordered their modest home where the trees had not yet fully leafed. Lilly described them as looking like lace this time of year, "like Mam's doilies," she said. Heddy had inherited the crocheted and tatted linens from her grandmother, Mam, after she died.

Heddy found peace in the woods, comforted there by her elders—the oaks and the maples. The lower storey of dogwood and sassafras trees were the first to flower and leaf in spring and blazed maroon and amber in the early fall. Living beneath this grand canopy, she visited it daily, hoping to absorb a mere dewdrop of nature's wisdom to guide her through her parenting day. Whenever Heddy walked here the throbbing of her heart slowed and her thoughts quieted enough that she could feel the wind brush her hair and smell the mushroomy dankness of loam and bark. Every parent should have a woods, she thought. The stillness and solitude of a copse of trees (even when they're not) settles even the antsiest of souls.

Friday evening, after Heddy, Joe, and Lilly dropped Ben at a friend's house for the evening, Lilly spotted a boy pedaling Ben's stolen bicycle in the parking lot of the old Sears store on Shelbyville Road. Kids often biked and skated there, now that the store was out of business. The parking lot made for an adequate, if too flat, skate park.

"Look, it still has all Ben's stuff on it. The dork hasn't even tried to disguise it." Lilly pointed to the trick pegs on the rear wheel and the handlebars wrapped with day-glo Bobolat that Ben also used to encase the grip of his tennis racquet.

Heddy lurched against her seatbelt as Joe wheeled the old Volvo across two lanes of traffic. He entered the parking lot, pulled up next to the boy, and asked him to wait. Joe spoke to the boy whose eyes searched the asphalt for answers. Joe put the bicycle in the back of the wagon, and the boy got in the backseat with Lilly. He'd told him he wanted to explain to his parents what had happened. Lilly slid as far to the right as she could, creating the maximum possible distance between herself and the alleged thief.

The boy, who was Ben's age, stared at his knees. He smelled like Ben and his buddies after a day of ball playing and bike riding. It was a mixture of souring sweat and chlorophyll.

"He claims he bought it from another kid for twenty bucks," Joe whispered as he drove.

The boy spoke only to give Joe his address, even then he mumbled. He had to repeat it twice before Joe got it right. "Twenty-two Seventeen Everett Avenue."

The home was an ordinary looking brick house with pansies and impatiens drawing a dotted arc next to the sidewalk. The porch light beamed as if awaiting the boy's return—like it did at their own house.

Joe led as they ascended a wooden ramp that took them on a zigzag route to the porch. You'd have thought the boy would have thrown open the door and raced inside hollering, "Mom, Dad," seeking parental protection from the stranger accompanying him. That's what Ben or Lilly would've done. Instead he just stood there with his hands pushed deep into pockets, sneaking nervous glances at Joe and shifting from one worn-down Nike to the other. Joe rang the bell.

A man that Heddy assumed was the boy's father finally opened the door. He was sitting in a wheelchair, and his flat stare gave her the impression that he was put out by the intrusion. Joe reached his hand out to the man, then retracted it, unshaken. Heddy knew Joe would be careful not to blame the boy who looked like he didn't have the gumption to steal second base, much less a bike.

Looking at the boy's father, she thought how unfair it was for people in wheelchairs to be stationed so far below eye level of everyone else. They ought to make them taller, she thought. No wonder he didn't want to shake hands, he would've had to reach up like a child.

Joe pulled out his wallet and handed the boy money, she assumed it was the twenty dollars the boy said he'd paid for the bike. The man looked from the boy to Joe and back to the boy. Heddy gasped when she saw the man snatch the cash from the boy's fist. "I wasn't going to keep it," the boy said, looking wrongly accused. She wondered if he meant the bike or the money.

"I think he goes to Ben's school," Lilly spoke without taking her eyes off the activity on the porch.

The man wheeled himself around and rolled back inside the house. The abruptness of his actions made him seem affronted and doubly humiliated by the episode. Through the open car window Heddy could hear the music for *Walker, Texas Ranger* blaring from a television. She was familiar with the music as this had been one her dad's favorite TV shows in his last years. The boy, his hands again shoved in his pockets, wagged his gelled head. He followed the man inside and shut the door, silencing the theme song. Left alone on the stranger's front porch, head hung low with one hand resting on his slouched hip, Joe looked for all the world like a rebuffed Bible salesman.

He reversed his path down the ramp, his tennis shoes slapping each plank in retaliation for their existence. He got back in the car, grumbling, "Nice to meet you too, asshole. Dad's the silent type."

"Maybe he was just embarrassed that his son got caught, and then there's that whole wheelchair thing." Heddy said. "He probably gave the boy the money in the first place."

After a pause, Joe continued, "I could see the kid after he went in the house. He was glaring at me from the couch. He looked trapped, like I'd taken away his only means of escape . . . poor kid."

Joe shrugged. It was a move that made Heddy think he was trying to shake off the entire incident—all of it: Ben's negligence, the man's seeming insolence, the boy's misery, his own guilt. It was something Heddy couldn't do. She would silently stew on every aspect for days, weeks even. Why hadn't the man spoken to the boy or to Joe? What if he couldn't? Could it have something to do with the wheelchair? . . . on and on, she'd ponder these and other questions. She both envied and resented Joe's ability to shrug things off so easily. She saw it equally as a gift and a curse.

That Sunday, with his bike returned, Ben didn't need to ask for a ride to tennis practice. He was grounded from riding it for two weeks outside of when it was deemed "necessary."

With Ben at practice all morning, Heddy and Joe and Lilly drove to their favorite lake, dubbed "Turtle Lake" by Lilly because of its inhabitants, and paddled around in a yellow canoe. They did this almost every Sunday the weather permitted. Heddy missed Ben being with them, imitating the croaks of the frogs with forced burps and worse.

Lilly pointed to every tiny turtlehead that broke the water's surface. Aside from the splash of the oars, the occasional plop of a frog, and squeal of a hawk, an uncommon quiet settled on them today like an early morning fog hovering vulnerably over the water. Heddy was sandwiched by Lilly in front and Joe in the rear, they each lay back, one against the other, like turtles on a log, floating, letting the subtle sways entrance them. It reminded her of the endless lazy afternoons she'd spent in her dad's garage in Gray Hampton.

Heddy rummaged the musty steamer trunks in the attic of her mind, still trying to make sense of the boy and the man. She wished that Joe hadn't automatically labeled him an *asshole* just from what he'd seen that night. Who knew his life? Didn't he walk the same tightrope that she did? But the way the boy hesitated to go inside his own house had really baffled her. It's just not what a kid would do.

A nudge on her back and Joe's voice brought her back to the present, "Time to go, Ben'll be home soon."

They pulled the canoe out of the water and turned it upside down on the rack that had been built to store it and others. Lilly slid the oars onto the canoe's cross bars. Heddy packed up their left-over lemonade and carrot sticks and Pringles and they headed back toward town.

"There wasn't even a hint of a breeze out there today," Joe said. "We had to do all the work ourselves. Lilly, did you ever see the lake that calm before?"

She shook her head.

"What did it look like to you?" he asked. "Close your eyes and tell me what you saw out there."

Lilly closed her eyes for what seemed like a blink, then said the lake looked "like the green glass of those old-fashioned 7-UP bottles that Gram Sal used to collect." Heddy smiled, having expected her to say it looked like glass or a mirror or some other overused simile. Joe taught elementary school in the next county and he enjoyed giving Ben and Lilly riddles to think through.

The country road they took to get to and from the lake was two-lane and paved and cut through farmland, mostly. No corn had sprouted yet, only flimsy tobacco sets speckled the soil. The land rolled in neat rows of red clay mounds and grassy patches that carpeted the deeper gullies where pooled rain might drown young crops. Since it was Sunday, traffic was sparse.

"I think I'll fix spaghetti for supper," Heddy said. It was Ben's favorite.

"Butter and cheese on mine, please," Lilly said as though her mother needed the reminder.

Then as Heddy reached for the radio knob to turn up the sound, she scanned the road and that's when she saw it.

"My God, Joe! What's that in the road?" she shaded her eyes from the sun. "It's a baby!" She blinked to improve her focus not trusting her vision; maybe it was her imagination.

But there, toddling right up the middle of the oncoming lane was a baby, barely walking—not yet two, wearing no shoes or clothes, only a diaper. Joe pulled the car onto the shoulder, and Heddy jumped out to rescue the baby right as a car was approaching in the distance.

The baby reached its arms toward her when Heddy got close

and whimpered what sounded like, "Up." Heddy looked around for anyone who might have seen her grab the baby, who might think she was stealing it.

How could a baby get here by itself, she wondered? In the car with the nameless child on her lap, Heddy flashed on Ben when he was this age. She looked around for a house or a car or a person. Streaks of dirt mixed with dried tears striped the baby's cheeks, he had tar-black feet and hands. He was jabbering and clawing at Heddy's face.

"Looks like a boy. What's your name little fella?" She rubbed his baldhead. "What do we do now, Joe?" Lilly sat forward and took one of the baby's hands in hers.

"I see a house about a quarter-mile up on the left," Joe steered the Volvo back onto the road.

He slowly turned the car into the gravel driveway. Heddy saw a man lift his head and look in the direction of the crunching gravel. Before that, his head had been stuck under the hood of a rusting Chevy pick-up. She noticed a long gun hanging across the rack in the truck's back window. It was parked at an awkward angle under an elm. Heddy figured the man must have pushed it there to work on it out of the sun. A small country house, white, with more wood showing than paint, stood next to the driveway.

A woman came around the corner from the back of the house, tossing a cigarette butt on the ground and talking on a wireless phone. Heddy got out of the car carrying the baby. She could feel her heart thumping even in her ears. She automatically slammed the door and looked back at it, wishing she had left it open.

The woman, thin with long dark hair, wore cut-off jeans and a shirt you could see clear through—a sheer white thing with puffy sleeves and a dark bra underneath it. She was pretty in that plain, bored way some women look. Heddy glanced back and saw Lilly and Joe with their eyes fixed on the woman.

Still talking on the phone, she walked toward Heddy. She looked neither at her nor at the baby. Heddy heard her say, "He just better get that fucking truck running so I can get me some cigarettes. I'll be a bitch and a half if I run clean out." The woman said this as she reached her free hand out for the baby as though she wanted Heddy to put him down on the ground. It was on gravel, for God's sakes.

"He was out in the middle of the road about a quarter-mile down," Heddy held the child tighter. "He could have been killed."

At that, the woman, though still engaged in conversation about the "fucking truck and cigarettes," grasped the baby's upper arm and lowered him to the gravel. Heddy had no choice but to release her grip to prevent a Solomon-like tug-of-war. The woman turned around and walked away as though she'd just dropped a sack of potatoes into her grocery cart. She gave him a restrained swat on the diaper as if to hurry him toward the back of the house . . . away from Heddy. It seemed like the baby knew her as he responded to her whack on his behind with a wobbly baby waddle.

"You ought to check his feet," Heddy called. "They're probably sore from the hot asphalt!"

She stood with her hand half reaching into the air from when she had let him go, still looking in the direction of the woman and the baby. She wasn't sure she shouldn't snatch him back or at least try again to talk to her. She caught movement out of the corner of her eye. The man had moved to the side of the truck and was staring at her with his arms folded in a way that conveyed he wasn't to be messed with. Joe tooted the horn and called to her. She walked back to the car and got in.

"What the hell just happened here? Do you think I should've just let her take that baby? She never even got off the phone; didn't act like she was relieved he was back, say thank you, or even kiss my ass. She was talking to somebody about running out of cigarettes." Heddy wrinkled her forehead and opened and closed her mouth as though she couldn't find the right words to express her bewilderment.

"Seems like it's probably happened before, the way neither of them acted upset or anything," Joe said. "I thought you were going to say she was on the phone to the police or somebody about her missing kid."

The man, who she assumed was the baby's father, had walked away from the truck and now stood ten feet in front of their car in the middle of the driveway, glaring at them like they might have been kidnappers. He wore coveralls with words, maybe a name, stitched above the pocket—ones like her father had worn to work on cars.

"I think we'd better go," Joe said as he maneuvered the driveway. "This guy could be trouble."

"If looks could kill . . . ?" Heddy said.

"That man is scary," Lilly said. "I think y'all ought to report them to the police."

Heddy watched the man in the side mirror. He stood watching them—one hand on his hip and the other in his pocket.

"Maybe when we get home we will, honey," Heddy said, rubbing her brow and cursing quietly. "She never said a word to me. I tried to tell her where we found him, but she just ignored me. Lilly, look and see if you can find a house number or anything."

Heddy considered that maybe the baby knew what he was doing by getting away in the first place, but she thought better of saying it in front of Lilly. She could see the man still watching them. She didn't relax until the station wagon went over the crest of a hill, putting the man out of sight.

Back home, Heddy filled two glasses with tap water and handed one to Joe. "What a weekend," she said. "First Ben's bike, but this baby . . . do you think we should do more?"

"Like what?" Joe asked.

"I don't know. Can't we still report her?"

"I deal with this kind of thing at school all the time. I doubt it would do any good—just cause us a big hassle. Did you notice any bruises on him?"

Ben rushed through the door, and made a mad dash for the fridge.

Joe took advantage of Ben's arrival to change the subject. "I'll need you to help me in the yard today, Benj."

"What's there to eat?" Ben scavenged inside the refrigerator. He held up a zip-lock of leftover pizza. "Can I have this?"

"Go ahead. You wouldn't be in the mood for spaghetti later, would you?" This was a moot question as Ben was always in the mood for any kind of pasta smothered with tomato sauce and topped with mounds of cheese. "How was practice?" She gave him as much of a hug as he would tolerate.

"Like always. Dad, can we look at those racquets sometime? I need a new one bad."

Joe shrugged and opened the door to go outside. "When you're finished eating, come help me move this table and chairs to the deck. It just gets in the way of the basketball hoop here."

There it was again, Joe shaking it off like he was finished with the matter entirely. It didn't seem like he was nearly as concerned about the two events, nor the recent changes she'd seen in Ben as she was.

One minute Ben would ask, "Can we go to the Custard Cup?" Then when they were loaded in the car, he'd refuse to go. "It's normal," Joe said. "It's because we're all going—like a family. He's afraid his friends will see him and tease him." Only having lived with sisters, Heddy assumed she just didn't understand boys.

Joe and Ben raked and mowed while Heddy and Lilly planted flowerpots with impatiens and petunias and marigolds. Heddy held up handfuls of the rich compost for Lilly to smell. Lilly made a face, but the odor of the mossy mix brought back memories to Heddy of planting pots with her grandmother Mam when she was Lilly's age. She and Lilly stacked the blooming crocks, almost twenty of them, all around the patio and on the back deck.

Heddy felt justified in judging the baby's mother more harshly than she had the boy's father. After all a toddler had been allowed to wander off into the road where god knows what could've happened. Was she turning into her mother, a circumstance she had always feared? Did she think mothers should be held to a higher standard or maybe it was simply because she was a mother and, therefore, identified more with the woman than the man. If you looked at it one way, things had turned out okay: they'd gotten Ben's bike back and rescued the baby from being hit by a car or lost in the woods. But she couldn't let it go at that. Both parents' lack of visible concern or relief made Heddy's uncertainty and lack of confidence in her own parenting glare like words plastered accusingly on a marquee. If only someone could give her answers. Her own mother had died a few years ago, so Heddy couldn't consult her; not that she wanted to. But Joe's mother, now she had all the answers as though they were as obvious as the proverbial bear in the woods. The woods, yes there it was, at least Heddy had the woods.

Her sisters had done their best to make Heddy afraid of the forest and its darkness. In Gray Hampton, the woods behind their house, at some indistinct dividing line, became the property of Essie Peck, who, it was said, would shoot at you for setting a single toe on her property. Most times Heddy was too absorbed in the scarred beeches and spindly cedars that bowed and weaved like sparring fighters to worry about such lore. The times she and her sisters had spotted the old woman, she was weeding in her garden or digging potatoes. Still, they'd scream and run as though she'd fired a potato missile at them.

Heddy stood cross-legged as Lilly positioned and re-positioned the plants. That back patio was huge, and it was rimmed by tall trees already heavy with pale green leaves. The patio overlooked a deep ravine, crisscrossed with two dead trees that had fallen years ago. Ben and his buddies would challenge each other to races across the fallen trunks. She'd seen them a couple times out the window, grinning and wobbling with their arms outstretched perpendicular to the tree's length like tight-rope acrobats. She'd held her breath until they made it across, but not wanting to seem over-protective, she said nothing.

She had to agree with Lilly that the ravine looked like lace this time of year with the still-blooming dogwoods mixed in with the taller trees. Lilly brought Heddy out of her melancholy by asking her mother to admire the arrangement of the flowers. "Perfect," Heddy said. The two of them had cut short branches of both the pink and the white dogwood blossoms for vases indoors. The blooms, with their sky-turned faces, made for simple, sparse, Asian-style arrangements. They had decorated their kitchen countertop and table every spring since the family had moved there.

Near four o'clock, Heddy called out as she sat in one of the chairs of the recently moved porch set, "I have a fresh deck of cards. Does anybody have some quarters they'd like to lose?"

Ben was the first to arrive. Heddy dealt the cards for a game of Skat. They got through about half the deck when Lilly plopped down in a chair next to her mother. Heddy included Lilly in the next hand.

Lilly started winning.

"Dad," Ben shouted. "Come play Skat with us. She cheats." He pointed at Lilly.

"I do not." Lilly slapped both hands flat on the table, her eyes wide at being so wrongly accused, as though she'd never cheated a day in her life.

Heddy was telling Ben about the baby they'd found that morning when Joe joined the game.

"His mom had on a see-through shirt." Lilly giggled through her cards. "You could see her bra."

"You could see her bra." Ben mocked his sister. "So?"

"It is so weird how neither the father of the boy with Ben's bike nor the mother of the baby said a single word to dad or me, or even to their kids." Heddy's own stepfather, Louis, had been a quiet man, but she felt sure that even he would have had some kind of response; if only a nod or a "thank you."

Ben squirmed when she brought up his bike. When she asked him if he knew the boy, he said he thought he did and then lifted himself up and backwards with both hands so he could sit on the rail that framed the deck. He rested his feet on the table and leaned forward with his elbows on his knees, one fist under his chin and the other fanning his cards.

"Get down, son," Joe said.

Heddy watched Ben fidget uncomfortably on the rail. He shifted his shoulders like his back itched and stared too long at his cards. At that second she became convinced that Ben had been the one who'd sold the boy his own bike.

But why? Ben loved that bike. She stood up to go get some tea and snacks from the kitchen as she finished her thought, "I just can't get it out of my head. Neither of them spoke a single word."

"The boy was a real dork," Lilly said, laying down the two of clubs. "But the baby was so cute."

"Ben, get your butt off there, you're making me nervous." She left the sliding door open. The sound of a radio announcing eighty-seven degree temperatures drifted outside, an abnormally warm temperature for this time of year.

Once again she'd exaggerated, she thought, thinking that Ben would have sold his Predator, especially for a mere twenty dollars. The bike was worth ten times that much. Besides, Ben had money that he'd earned from his paper route. Heddy shrugged, hoping to shake off her guilt over falsely accusing him. She smirked, thinking it must only work for men, or maybe only Joe. What if he had, though? What if he was being bullied or pressured? She needed to ask him about it.

She was gone less than five minutes. As she approached the open doors with a fresh pitcher, she could hear Ben gloating about beating both Joe and Lilly. Most of the quarters lay on the table in front of him. Sure, she thought, it's easy to win when you can see everybody else's cards, as he was still perched on the wooden slat, giving him a birds-eye view of both Joe's and Lilly's hands.

She tried not to pick at her children, to save it for the important things. Then, she wondered what the important things might be; this issue with the bike was definitely an important thing.

"After I win this hand, how about I crush you in a game of horse, Dad?"

"You're on." Joe held up his hand for a high-five.

At that moment the muscles in Heddy's gut contracted involuntarily. Something was badly wrong on this windless day. Either the house was slowly turning sideways or she was experiencing vertigo. She sensed movement, she just couldn't tell what or where. It was a feeling she sometimes had in the car on long trips when she'd be suddenly awakened by the car veering sharply.

The air was as still as the dust on a table, not a leaf waved. Then she heard a familiar slow-motion cracking; a sound she'd heard before during bad storms, and she knew immediately what it was. She knew what was happening.

She dropped the tray of food and screamed, "Ben get off the damned rail!" She lunged at him at the same time the falling tree slammed across the corner of the deck. She grabbed for Ben's feet, but her hands only grazed the toes of his tennis shoes that, by then, stuck straight up as he somersaulted backwards into thin air.

The tree hit the bottom of the thirty-foot ravine with a thud that shook them like an earthquake. Blood oozed from Heddy's forehead where a branch had grazed it.

After that, nothing—no sound, no movement. The radio announcer's voice had gone dead. Even the constant drone of the air conditioner had quit.

The right-hand corner of the deck and the rail were splintered and gone, and so was her son. Lilly screamed, "Ben!"

"Get help!" Heddy shrieked as she slid down the embankment into the ravine. Her shirt clung to a jagged branch that gashed her arm. She felt no pain, only the need to get to Ben as fast as she could, to pull him from under the tree, to hold him against her like she had the baby earlier that very day.

She heard Joe shouting directions to their house, "fifteen zero eight Myrtle," into the phone and begging them, "please hurry." Then he was beside her. "Lilly, go watch for them out front." He tried to sound calm.

The tree had snagged an electrical wire as it fell. Heddy surveyed the full trunk and the dangling wire, the tree bisected Ben's stomach and chest at an angle. "We'll get this off you, buddy." They shoved and pushed, but no amount of heaving would budge the wood off him. Joe grabbed Heddy's hand as she reached for the wire.

The next thing she knew, Joe was motioning to several men and women in uniforms. "Down here," he shouted, then "Stay up there, Lilly." But Lilly slid down the hill anyway.

Joe grabbed hold of Lilly and Heddy tightly to keep them out of the way of the EMTs and firemen, or to steady himself, slipping as he stood on a bank of leaves and mud. He edged Heddy and Lilly away from Ben. Heddy heard sobbing, but Ben's face was stock-still.

The tree must have clipped one of the dogwood trees as white blossoms lay next to Ben's face. He'd landed on a bed of rotting leaves and moss. The sweet dank mulch gave off the same scent as the pots she'd planted earlier with Lilly.

The uniforms squatted next to Ben with their silver cases gaping. One man used a hook to move the electrical wire; another put his fingers on Ben's wrist and on his neck; a woman put her whole mouth over Ben's and squeezed his nose. "Can you get at his chest?" one uniform said to the other. He shook his head. After several minutes, they sat back on their haunches and glanced at the other, then at Heddy and at Joe with helpless and hopeless eyes.

She wished they would leave. She would dig him out with her bare hands. She wrenched away from Joe. She reached across the fallen trunk and brushed leaves and mulch and dogwood petals from her son's perfect face and hair. *I shouldn't have screamed at him.*

Heddy became convinced—obsessed—that she had been the cause of her son's falling. She thought she must have startled him when she screamed, making him lose his balance. There wasn't one person to whom she could confess this regret. No one would believe her anyway, she thought—probably call her irrational. Reason, like religion, was not a concept she relied upon anymore. Not that she considered religion reasonable, but an archetype in which she no longer believed, nor trusted; an entity in which she did not place her faith.

When children being raised in the Catholic tradition attain their seventh birthday, it is said they have reached "the age of reason," meaning that now they must take responsibility for their actions, they are capable of sinning, they know right from wrong. Heddy knew well the sins she had committed since her seventh birthday, but reason had nothing to do with her culpability, guilt, or atonement for her offenses. So, labeling herself as irrational seemed as accurate a description as any.

Was it not irrational that a goddamned tree had fallen without even the slightest urging? She couldn't get the image of the tree crashing and of Ben tumbling backwards out of her mind. However, it was not horror that Heddy suffered with—it was guilt, regret, remorse, and self-condemnation combined with an emptiness that would never, should never, she thought, go away. It was desolation and hopelessness. It was utter despair—one of the deadly seven.

THE SORRY CABIN

The three of us, Joe, Lilly, and me, were lined up on the couch like disobedient children, as the investigators explained their "ruling," that Ben's death was an accident. They told us how and why Ben died, as if they'd been there when it happened.

I tried to listen. They said the tree, an ash, was practically hollow at the base. "Rotted from the inside out." Yet it had leafed out almost completely, and then snapped right at the ground on a day without even the slightest wind.

"It's not unusual," the other added. "Its falling was just a matter of time, not wind."

They stayed for over an hour.

I quit listening.

Once they left, I looked at Joe and said, "Not unusual?" Then thought as I left the room: not unusual that a perfectly healthy looking tree fell on a completely windless day right at the same time Ben chose to sit on the railing of the deck. Not unusual that we hardly ever sat on that deck.

It'd been weeks since our son's death and I was numb—not angry, not crying. It seemed like the investigators had been describing me—that I was the thing that was hollow; that I was rotting inside, and that time or wind would soon break me.

Joe seemed to know that there were chores that needed to be done. I could hear him doing things while I stared out the kitchen window. I looked at the chickadees and nut hatches on the feeder and the flowers that Lilly and I had planted, but all I saw was a tree falling onto the deck and Ben tumbling backwards off the rail. Lilly was to and fro between Joe and me, one minute stoic and the next a pond of tears. Sometimes she would sit in my lap and cry and then other times she would talk about Ben in ways that I couldn't yet. "Remember how Ben would stand on his bed and use his coat rack as a microphone. Then he'd lip sync *Stairway to Heaven*. What a nerd."

A few weeks later, I heard Joe call Lilly out to the garage. I walked out with her. I sat in a lawn chair and watched them roll Ben's white dirt bike into the middle of the floor. Joe reattached the kickstand that Ben had taken off, while Lilly unwrapped the green tennis racquet tape from the handlebars. Then they washed the bike with soapy water.

"I thought we'd give Ben's bike back to that kid in the Highlands," Joe said.

"The look on the kid's face the night we took it away from him makes me think he could really use it. I'll put a note on it and leave it on his front porch. Want to come?"

Lilly did, but I didn't.

"What will you say in the note?" I asked.

Joe shrugged.

"I thought I'd put something like, 'Ben would want you to have this,' unless you want me to write something else."

"No, sounds fine."

"Are you going to ask him for the twenty bucks?" Lilly asked.

Ben had failed to lock his bike at tennis practice one morning and it was stolen. When we happened upon this boy riding it, he told us he'd bought it for twenty dollars. Joe took the bike from the boy and gave him twenty dollars in return.

"No, I don't want it back."

Joe and Lilly loaded the bike into the Volvo and left, and I went back to my chair in the kitchen. Cooking crossed my mind, but I couldn't seem to find the strength to actually prepare any food. Clementine jumped into my lap. The muted calico purred and kneaded my thighs getting comfortable.

I looked at the woods bordering our home that had once been such a comfort. I walked there daily, seeking and sorting—questions, answers; quiet. But, now they'd betrayed me—one of them killed Ben. Trees have always felt spiritual and wise, especially the grand old oaks, beeches, and pines. Sitting among them I could hear their voices as their limbs and leaves quivered with the least breeze. I missed those woods, those crones, almost as much as I missed Ben.

I was no help to Joe or Lilly. I was too weighed down by the tree that lay on my chest. It held me down. It kept me in one spot. I knew Joe and Lilly needed me, but I couldn't help them, or myself. The more I realized how much they hurt, the more I couldn't move.

I made a decision. It wasn't a decision based on reason or discernment. It was a decision that grew from need.

After delivering the bike, Joe and Lilly walked in with a pizza that smelled like pepperoni and hot cardboard. "How'd it go?"

Joe sat the pizza on the table and pulled out a chair to sit down. "The kid was in the front room, I guess watching television. He must have seen us out on the porch because he came outside. He said he'd heard about Ben from some of the boys from their school . . . said he was sorry."

Lilly got plates out and set the table. She filled glasses with water and placed them at each plate. She climbed up on the counter to get the salt and the napkins out of the higher cabinets.

"Careful, honey," I said.

"Lilly rolled the bike over to him like she was handing it to him, and he looked at me. I said, 'Take it, we want you to have it.' He took the bike from Lilly and said thanks and rubbed his hand across the seat. Lilly told him he might want to take that kickstand off. Then she remembered the lock and chain we'd left in the car. I asked him if he wanted me to say something to his dad and, not a surprise, he declined my offer. He followed us down the ramp to the car to get it; and Lilly and I left. That was it!"

Joe and Lilly ate two or three slices apiece. "We never gave him the note Dad wrote," Lilly said.

"Did you get his name?" Joe shrugged his shoulders. I wrapped up the left over slices and took the empty box to the recycling bin in the garage. I put the dishes and silverware in the dishwasher and sat back down. The sun sank as I waxed melancholic, unsure even of what day of the week it was. I heard the TV come on. It sounded like a movie.

It took nearly another month for me to talk to Joe about my decision. So much had changed between us since the accident. It was my fault. Joe tried everything he could think of to help me—fixing meals, taking me for rides, to movies. We had always been friends first, and lovers second. And, even though we had plenty of friends, we were just as content to hang out with each other. I didn't know if we'd ever get that back, but it wouldn't be for the lack of Joe trying. He'd suggested that we take a trip somewhere out west or "wherever you'd like to go," he said.

"I can't go on a trip. I can't pretend to be okay. Sitting in this chair is just about all I can muster."

It was August and still hot even at dusk. After Lilly went to bed,

Joe sat down with me in the kitchen.

"I think I'm going to move into the Sorry Cabin for a while," I said.

My parents had left us the cabin. It wasn't much more than a shack, really. When Joe saw it the first time, he said, "This is the sorriest cabin I believe I've ever seen." And the name stuck.

We hadn't used the cabin much since the kids were born. It was buried deep in the woods and surrounded by farms. It was in the boondocks outside of of Gray Hampton, the town where I was raised. When it rained or snowed, you needed a four-wheel drive vehicle to get to and from it. If it'd had a lake or a barn for horses, the kids might have liked it better. But for them, it was boring.

"What about Lilly? You can't just go off and leave her. She doesn't need to lose anybody else."

I imagined Lilly asleep in her room. She was on the small side of average with brown eyes and hair. Her hair was fine and when she was a baby it stood straight up like my grandfather's crew cut. When she woke up in the mornings her hair looked as though she'd been riding around all night in a convertible—with the top down and no scarf. Ben teased her constantly about her bed-head.

"I'll call her every day. I'll call you both. It'll have to be better than her seeing me like this all the time. Watching the two of you day in and day out and having to look at Ben's room and these woods, I can't seem to think about anything else. Maybe if I'm alone for a while I can start to sort things out."

"Lilly's too young to understand why you're going. You can't do this to her, not now."

"We're all hurting, even you, but I see you and Lilly able to go on with your lives. That tree might have fallen on Ben, but it feels like it's sitting on my chest all day, every day. I've got to get it off me. This is the only thing I can think to do."

He pulled me into his lap and wrapped his arms around me. "I miss Ben, but I miss you, too. I miss us. I'm afraid you won't come back."

At breakfast the next morning, I wasn't prepared for Lilly's reaction.

"Mom and I have something to tell you, Lil. Mom's decided to go away for a while."

Before either of us could say any more, Lilly threw down her spoon and bawled, "Are you getting a divorce?" She looked at me and said, "You are the most selfish person in the world. I hate you." She took off out the back door and slammed it hard.

Joe started after her, but I stopped him. "Let me," I said. I found her on the back deck. She was breathing hard, but not crying. She was standing right where the tree had hit only two months before.

"Dad and I aren't getting a divorce, but you're right about me being selfish. That's why I think it would be better for me to go away and be by myself for a while. To try to stop being so selfish so I can act like your mom again." I heard her breathing slow, and she turned and looked at me. She actually let me hug her and pick her up and carry her back inside.

We all sat back down to our cereal and toast.

"Is that cabin in any shape for you to live in?" Joe asked.

"What cabin? Do you mean the Sorry Cabin? You're going to stay in the Sorry Cabin? That place is awful."

"Why don't we ride out there today and take a look at it," Joe said.

Lilly seemed to accept the idea of my leaving for a while once she knew I would just be out at the Sorry Cabin.

It was basically one big room with a kitchen on one end and a big stone fireplace on the other. There was a tiny room next to the bathroom that you might be able to fit a double bed in. The only things it had going for it were the fireplace and the windows. It had lots of windows that looked out onto mossy ground that was interspersed with pines and oaks and hemlocks.

"All I'll have to do is get a phone, turn the water back on and fill the propane tank." Joe and I surveyed the room.

"Well, you might need a little furniture," he said.

"Not really. I'll just take a few things from the house."

"You can use my bed if you want." Lilly offered.

I hadn't been this active in over a month. It tired me out. On the ride back home, I tried to remember what life had been like before the accident. It seemed so far away—like another lifetime. Even the old Volvo station wagon was different. Whenever we went on trips Lilly would sit in the back seat, and since Ben was the oldest, he called dibs on the "way-way," as he named it. We kept a quilt back there for him to lie down on. There was a shoebox of games he played with. All of it was still in the back of the wagon. Ben had hated this car. He was embarrassed by it. He called it the "grocery getter" and the "cheese mobile." He wanted us to get something cool, like an SUV, or a Mustang, or at least, a van.

The next day I started gathering up what I thought would not be missed—a couple of mismatched towels and sheets, an old set of dishes, and some of my clothes. Joe and Lilly said they had something to do and left the house before noon.

I settled back into the kitchen chair and resumed watching out the windows and making a lap for Clementine. I thought about how Ben used to play when he was a baby. He'd sit for hours amid Fischer-Price people and blocks of wood with an entire saga going on within the confines of his mind. He'd make little squeaks and occasionally say actual words while he walked the people with his hands and knocked down stacks of blocks. He was probably re-enacting something he'd seen on Sesame Street or the Electric Company or Mister Rogers Neighborhood, but I really didn't know.

Lilly, on the other hand was much more of a doer, an extrovert. She liked company to play and interact with. She always talked to her dolls out loud. She talked and walked a lot earlier than Ben had. Whatever thought that popped into Lilly's mind usually came out her mouth.

About five o'clock Lilly and Joe came home. I hadn't noticed how much time had passed, but Joe apologized for having been gone so long.

"Where were you?" I suddenly remembered to ask.

"We went over to school. I wanted to work on my classroom a little before school starts. Lilly helped me out. You know how she likes to decorate the bulletin boards." Joe winked at Lilly.

Lilly carried bags from the Kroger deli. "We got you your favorite." Lilly pulled out a goldfish box that read pasta salad. She unpacked the rest of it and we ate as the sky turned from blue to black.

The following Saturday, Joe borrowed a truck from a fellow teacher. We packed all that I thought I needed in the station wagon and the truck. I saw Lilly load the cat carrier into the cab of the truck and crawl inside to ride with Joe for the forty-or-so mile drive to the Cabin. I drove the wagon.

They got there before I did. I stopped to pick up groceries to stock the kitchen. When I pulled up to the Sorry Cabin, I wondered what I'd likely forgotten. I gathered up as many bags as I could carry from the back and headed toward the door. I was halted by what I saw. Hanging from the front porch rafters was a brand new oak swing. They'd even bought a long, thick cushion for the seat. "Beautiful!" I actually smiled.

Joe and Lilly had almost everything unloaded from the borrowed truck and inside the house by the time I got there. Joe and I carried down an old couch we'd found at Goodwill. Lilly made iced tea, and we sat in the swing to rest. Joe pulled around an old unpainted Adirondack chair for himself.

"Mom!" Lilly said like she'd just realized it. "You don't have a TV!"

Joe and I laughed. It felt good to laugh and to have been distracted for a while. I heard rustling and looked toward the screen door and saw something furry and grayish sitting and looking out. It was Clementine.

"Dad said we could get a new kitten for home, maybe two," Lilly said.

"Thanks for letting Clemmie come with me. I'll try to take good care of her."

Joe stood up like it was time to go. "You're sure you'll be all right?" He put his arm around me. "Maybe you should wait until the phone is activated."

I shook my head. "I love the swing. Thanks."

Lilly asked if she could spend the night, then changed her mind when she remembered the TV situation. I waved and watched them pull away.

Three months to the day had passed since Ben died. I woke up that first morning at the cabin feeling hungry since I hadn't eaten any supper the night before. I fed Clementine and thought about breakfast. I was wearing one of Joe's old t-shirts that smelled like a mix of his aftershave and coffee; I call it "Joe and Joe." It was the scent of home and of morning when Joe gets up before me to make the coffee and to shower. He brings two cups to bed and reads me the sports pages. I could not have felt more gloomy or more alone at this moment and wondered why I'd left, why I thought this could ever help.

"Okay Heddy, all you have to do is pour cereal and milk in a bowl," and I dug a bowl and a spoon out of one the boxes.

After breakfast, I wandered out onto the porch and sat down in the swing. I pulled my knees up inside my t-shirt against the morning chill. The cold skin felt good against my chest. I turned sideways and leaned with my back against the chains. I wondered what Ben would think about me going off like this. He'd be too young to understand it. What he'd say would not likely be what he felt. He didn't like to hurt my feelings, but I think he'd think it was a cop-out.

Ben's social studies class had studied the War in Vietnam this past school year. When he realized that Joe hadn't gone to Desert Storm or Vietnam, and why, he'd been disappointed. Joe tried to explain how he didn't feel it was right to kill another person, even in war. "Anyway, I'm too old to have fought in Desert Storm," Joe said.

"What about all those other guys who had to?" Ben asked. "What about the ones that died over there?"

"I was against the war entirely," Joe said. "I never thought we should have gotten involved. Lots of people felt that way. We thought there were better ways to solve problems than killing innocent people."

"Were you one of those protesters?" Ben asked. "Did you spit on the soldiers who came home?"

"Of course I didn't. None of those guys went over there because they wanted to. Most of the ones who fought were against the war too. They did what they had to, just like me."

A few of the kids in his class told stories about their dad or mom who'd served in Desert Storm. The stories must have made the soldiers sound heroic and exciting. I worried because it seemed like Ben saw Joe differently after that. Joe said that he too had thought of war as exciting when he was Ben's age. "The books make it seem that way. Ben's still too young to comprehend it all. It wouldn't be cool as a middle schooler to be against it."

I was ashamed of the relief I felt over not having to worry about Ben going off to war, or about him getting hurt in a car wreck or hurting someone else, or getting some girl pregnant. I felt the same relief in no longer having to struggle to come up with ways to parent him and in knowing what to say and do for him when his heart was broken. It was a quarrelsome feeling—relief and regret at the same time. I felt liberated on the one hand and was gnawed by anguish, grief, and remorse on the other. I would've given anything to be wrapped inside the struggles and the anxieties of raising that dear sweet boy.

"You don't have to worry anymore, because he's already dead. How perverse is that?" I was on the verge of losing my soul along with my mind.

By noon, it was turning into a typical late August day in Kentucky—hot and humid—with a chance of rain. The cabin stayed cool because of the trees that overhung the roof. I studied all the ones visible from the swing. I wondered if any were hollow or rotten on the inside. There were a few that I couldn't identify. The taller ones were oaks, and a huge sycamore stood next to the driveway. The spaces between the taller trees were filled in with cedars and hemlocks. Closer to the ground grew large clumps of jewelweed and leggy forsythia and prickly blackberry bushes. The birds had feasted on most of the berries, but there were still a few left to pick.

I walked around the outside of the cabin. The lack of care it had received since my parents died was clearly apparent. Its wood plank siding had never been painted. The boards had turned gray but none were warped. For some reason they'd put on wood shake shingle roof, and in this shady environment it made a perfect host for moss and lichen and purple bird shit.

The place looked scruffy, yet solid and well built. I completed my inspection and reverted to the swing. The cushion that Joe and Lilly had bought for it was brightly colored. It was yellow and red and purple, a stark contrast to the dull gray cabin. The pillow stood out as boldly as a cardinal in a field of fresh snow.

I spent my days scouring and surveying the area, but mostly reclining in the swing. Clemmie had found a way to get outside. She sat in the swing with me, and did as little as I did. I knew Lilly would not approve of her being outdoors. I could just hear her saying, "She's an indoor cat, Mom. She can't protect herself." She probably wouldn't think I was capable of protecting her either, and she'd be right. But Clementine didn't wander off and only came out if I was out.

□

It was the end of the first week, and everything I'd brought to the cabin was right where Joe and Lilly had left it. Even the couch sat facing the wall. I climbed over the arm at night to sleep on it. I hadn't bothered with pulling the hide-a-bed out. The only unpacking I'd done was out of necessity. Today I was searching for laundry soap. I needed to wash the t-shirt I'd worn all day and night since I'd changed for bed that first evening.

Laundry was another thing I hadn't been concerned with in months. I was beginning to realize how little I'd been able to do. There wasn't much I was doing at the cabin either, but I was, at least, beginning to see it.

The only thing I'd done for myself back home was bathe. Even though there was no one here to offend, I thought I'd better take a bath before I warded off the birds and squirrels. The water was hot, almost too hot, and the smell of the lavender soap was calming. I closed my eyes and slipped under the water. My pulse throbbed at my temples. It was the most serene I had felt in months. I stuck my nose out of the water enough to breathe and relaxed to the point of floating. I stayed this way until the water cooled.

Refreshed and revived in clean shorts and a shirt, I tackled the rat's nest that had overtaken my head. My hair was so snarled from lack of brushing, it took me half an hour to detangle the matted mess. It reminded me of Lilly. I looked in the mirror and was surprised at how long my hair had grown. I found scissors and shortened it a couple of inches. Once it was dry I pulled it up in a clip.

It hit me when I saw my reflection in the mirror just how long it had been since I'd really looked at myself. New wrinkles had formed around my eyes and mouth; ones I hadn't noticed before.

The phone rang as I walked out of the bathroom. It was Joe. "Looks like you've got a phone now. How are things going?"

"Fine, I guess. I just took my first bath. How'd you find my number?"

"MCI gave it to us the day we signed up."

"I hadn't even thought to check the phone. How are things at home? How's Lilly?"

"We're both fine. We thought we'd come out and see you sometime—you know school starts on Monday."

"Okay, just let me know before you come; not that I'm going anywhere."

The next morning the phone rang early.

"We're about to get in the car. Dad wants to know if you want us to bring you anything."

"I don't think so, at least I can't think of anything right now."

I heard the click of Lilly hanging up the phone.

"Shit." I knew they would be distressed to see things still the same. So I quickly dragged the couch around so that it faced the fireplace. I opened the windows and slid the unpacked boxes into the empty bedroom. It only took a minute to wash the few dishes I'd used, so I made tea and checked for ice. "What if they want something to eat?" I'd already gone through most of the groceries I'd brought. I searched one of the boxes for two more glasses and plates. Since there really weren't any cabinets to store the dishes, I set the table for lunch. Then I scooted the table over to the window so that it looked out onto the porch.

The dishes were ones Joe and I'd gotten as a wedding present. We hadn't used them in years. The sight of them brought back memories of an earlier, happier time. When we were first married, I was not the best cook. One night I attempted to prepare a meatloaf. I made it with Quaker Oatmeal instead of soda crackers. After it was cooked, the mixture of the meat and the red sauce with the oatmeal made the mound of meat turn a putrid green. We ate it any way. It didn't taste as bad as it looked. When he was finished Joe picked up his empty plate, one from this very set, and licked the remnants off it. How is it he always seemed to know what to do to make me feel better? I wished he could do that now.

As I washed a plate, I remembered one was missing. It happened during the first year we were married when Joe began talking about our starting a family. It was as though he couldn't stand for it to be just the two of us. He wanted a baby and he wanted it now. When I said for the umpteenth time that I was not ready for a baby and that I wouldn't be until I was out of school for at least a year, he threw the plate on the floor with two hands. "Then what the hell did we get married for?"

The subject could have cost us our marriage, early on. But after graduation, I was pregnant within six months.

□

Two car doors slammed, and then I heard two more. Surely they hadn't brought anyone with them. I looked out to see Lilly carrying a cat box and Joe with his arms around two grocery bags.

I held open the screen door.

"Wait till you see, Mom, just wait." Lilly sat the carrier on the floor. She opened the cage door but nothing emerged.

I looked inside to see four blue eyes in the far end of the carrier staring back at me.

"They're Siamese," she said as she pulled a frightened kitten from the box.

Clementine slinked over and smelled the one still inside and it smacked at her nose.

"They're beautiful." I took the kitten from Lilly. "When did you get them?"

"A few days ago. I wanted to be able to spend some time with them before school starts. Wouldn't Ben love them?"

Joe had unloaded the bags he brought—groceries and the fixings for lunch. He stood, arms folded, with his back to the sink and watched us. I looked over at him. "You are such a pushover."

"How do you like your new digs? I see you've tastefully arranged the couch and table."

I walked over and stood next to him at the sink. He hung his arm around my neck and kissed my cheek.

Joe made grilled Swiss cheese sandwiches on whole wheat. They tasted like a gourmet meal to me. I said, "I'm glad to see the stove works." Joe just shook his head. After lunch he and I strolled around the outside of the house. I pointed out the fuzzy roof and unhinged shutters. Lilly stayed inside with the kittens that she'd named George and Marcel. She said she tried to think of names for them that she thought Ben would have picked. Wandering the cabin, she must have discovered Clementine climbing out a hole in the bathroom screen. I found it later stuffed with a fat wad of toilet paper.

"Dad, it's almost two. We need to leave if we're going shopping."

"We're going back-to-school shopping today, but we have to take the kittens home first. You're welcome to join us. I'd bring you back tonight."

"I'll take a rain check. Maybe I could meet the two of you for supper one evening."

As much as I loved seeing them, I could hardly wait for them to leave. Having such a wishy-washy reaction to spending time with my husband and daughter made me wonder if I'd ever want to live with them as a family again. Every feeling emitting from my heart—my psyche—seemed to be countered with equal and opposite dizzying lunacy. My emotions were engaged in a war, one against the other, with neither bent on winning. Opposing sentiments arguing and agreeing with each other in the same instant. Symptoms likely included in the Manual of Mental Disorder's definition of insanity.

I walked them to the car.

"Oh, I almost forgot, here's some paint they were getting rid of at school. It's too bright for anything at home. But, I thought you might use it to brighten this place up a little."

I said thanks, having no intention of using it.

I spent the rest of the day and the week in the swing swaying back and forth just enough to stir up a breeze. I slept on the pullout couch, ate breakfast and dinner, bathed, called home, padded around the cabin and the woods, and sat in the swing again. It was my routine for weeks. At least it was more than I'd done at home. I even washed my clothes in the bathtub occasionally. Maybe that's why Joe was halfway willing for me to leave. He knew I'd have to take care of myself in the cabin.

My first thought every morning was still of a falling tree and of Ben tumbling backwards. Sometimes I even reached out with my arms and hands to grab his feet as they swung backwards over his head. But every time the white Adidas slipped right past my grasp. One morning I was almost out of bed before the thought arose.

On another warm morning in early October, I popped out of bed and strode directly to that can of paint Joe had brought. I didn't eat or brush my teeth or even change out of my t-shirt. It was as though some hypnotic or extraterrestrial force was drawing me. It took the breaking of two knives to get the can open. I stirred it with a stick and used a sponge from the sink for a brush. The color was almost the exact purple in the swing's cushion. When I was finished, the swing looked almost cheerful in its new lilac coat. The next day, I painted the Adirondack chair and the front door the same color.

When I went to the store later that day, I bought some yellow paint and brushes for the screen door.

With the cushion back in place, I couldn't help but smile at the combination. I admired my handiwork, then took a turn in the woods.

The next Saturday that Joe visited, he brought more paint, none of which had been opened. I figured when he'd heard that I'd painted the swing and the door, he'd bought it to keep me busy. I ended up with several gallons of a pale apple green paint—Ben's favorite color. He'd picked the same hue to paint his bedroom.

I contemplated the purple swing and door for three days. There were shutters on the windows that were falling apart. I repaired and painted them purple too until I ran out of purple paint and switched to yellow mid-shutter.

The next week, I bought fabric, thread, and needles for making curtains. Unlike the other women in my family, I'd never sewn a seam in my life. I don't know what I was thinking. It was just like painting the swing, as though someone, something, else had taken hold of my hands and brain. I measured and scissored and hemmed for a week and ended up with curtains for every single window. Clementine entertained herself and me by chasing loose threads and frayed fabric strands around the floor.

It was the following Friday evening that I met Joe and Lilly at the Bristol Bar and Grille in Middletown. I told them all about my stitching frenzy and sought sympathy for my needle-wounded fingertips. I asked them to come out when they had time to see.

Lilly talked about school and for the first time she asked me, "When are you coming home?"

"I don't know yet. Why?"

"Cause you may need to make new curtains for my room. George and Marcel have just about ruined mine. First Marcel climbs them chasing after a fly and then George takes off after her." Then as an afterthought, she asked, "Is Clementine still getting out?"

"No," I lied.

It was close to Lilly's birthday and I asked her if she'd like to bring some friends out to the Sorry Cabin for a sleep over. "You could roast marshmallows and hot dogs in the fireplace or maybe we could build a bonfire in the clearing."

"I'll think about it." She looked unconvinced.

I knew she was worried about what her friends would think about me not living at home. "You could tell your friends it's our weekend getaway cabin."

She nodded, intent on eating her noodles. When Lilly went to the bathroom, Joe said, "You're really looking great. Do you feel any better?"

"I think I'm starting to come out of it a little. I spent the entire day crying on Wednesday. It's actually the first time I've cried since the funeral."

Joe had tears in his eyes when he took my hand.

"How's school going?"

"It's not been my finest year. I've got a boy in my class who reminds me so much of Ben at that age I can hardly take my eyes off him. The resemblance is frightening.

"You remember the baby we found walking in the road the morning before the accident?" Joe asked.

I nodded.

"Last week Lilly gathered up a bunch of Ben's old books, toys, and baby clothes and asked if we could take them to that baby. I said I'd talk to you about it. I didn't think it'd be a very good idea to go back there alone with Lilly. Maybe, the three of us could go."

"Wow, she did that? I'll bring it up when she gets back. It's pretty bad when your nine-year-old daughter is braver than you are."

"I've come upon her in Ben's room going through his closet a couple of times. I haven't said anything about it. I've just sat down on the edge of his bed and talked about something else. I think she's OK, but you never know. At least she talks. She doesn't seem to keep things bottled up."

When Lilly came back I said, "Dad said you wanted to give some things to that baby out near the lake. When do you want to go?"

"What about Sunday?"

"That sounds good to me. I'll drive in to the house. I haven't seen the place for almost three months. Maybe it's time. Then we can drive out to the baby's house together. What did you pick to take?"

"Ben's Joey doll, a lot of books and some clothes—I saved his blanket and *Nightmare* book. The baby's mom didn't look like she'd be the type to buy him books."

The day we came upon the toddler in the road, his mother had seemed more concerned about running out of cigarettes and talking on the phone than about her baby almost getting killed. Lilly had been intrigued by how the woman was dressed. She'd worn really short shorts and a see-through shirt. I guess Lilly didn't think she looked like the motherly type.

"Dad and I both think it's a really good idea you've come up with."

They walked me to the station wagon, and I almost felt like going with them. "See you Sunday then. Around ten?"

Joe gave me a good long kiss through the open window. "I miss you." He didn't wait for a reply. The kiss was as soft and melting as eating a warm, sweet, roasted marshmallow. It was lovely to enjoy something again, especially kissing.

I spent Saturday in a funk. I regretted saying I would come to the house. I dreaded seeing the place again. I told myself I didn't have to go inside or to the back deck or look at the woods. I hoped I wouldn't start crying.

Swinging helped, but I still spent the whole day in my t-shirt and robe. The chill in the air made me wonder what I'd do when it was too cold to sit outside. Swinging had become my meditation. It helped free my mind of the tree. I no longer felt its weight on me, but I could still see Ben's broken body underneath it and the electrical wire a limb had snagged on its way down. It would be an image that would never leave me.

□

I pulled into the driveway next to Joe's ten-year-old Camry on Sunday and waited. Neither Joe nor Lilly came out. I lightly tooted the horn; still no sign of them, so I skulked inside through the garage and the kitchen door.

"Where are you guys?"

"Back here," Lilly answered.

I teetered down the long hallway that led to to our bedroom, Joe's and mine—past Lilly's and past Ben's. Lilly was standing on the bed with a worried look on her face, and Joe was in the closet bent over on his hands and knees. Lilly explained that George had accidentally gotten out, and when they opened the door for him to come in, he'd run in carrying a chipmunk in his mouth.

When Joe finally emerged from the closet he was holding George by the scruff. The chipmunk was wiggling in George's mouth. If Joe'd been a cougar or a coyote, it would've looked like a chart of the food chain. Joe took them both outside where the chipmunk managed to free itself. It limped off looking stunned.

Joe tossed George back inside. He had blood dripping from his forearm where George must have scratched him. I helped him clean it and put on a Band-Aid.

Lilly and I put the box she had packed with Ben's clothes, toys, and books in the back of the wagon and the three of us headed out. Being in the house had not been as awful as I'd imagined, as the chipmunk event had been a good-enough distraction.

Finding the baby in the road all those months ago had been frightening and upsetting at the time it happened. But then the tree fell, and I had hardly thought about the strange event since until Lilly brought it up. So it certainly seemed like it had been on her mind.

We pulled into the same driveway where we'd parked that day last May. Joe helped Lilly drag the box out of the back and the three of us approached the front door. Joe knocked. The baby's mother came to the door—quickly followed by the baby with a bottle in his mouth. He was dressed this time. He wore bib overalls and a t-shirt, but still no shoes or socks. The first time I hadn't really noticed his blue eyes or red hair. But it was the mother who really shocked me. She was smoking a cigarette and appeared to be about four or five months pregnant.

For some reason, it really aggravated me—her being pregnant—now she gets to totally screw up two innocent little kids. I wondered if Joe and Lilly noticed her slightly protruding belly.

Joe explained. "I don't know if you remember us or not, but we're the people who found your little boy wandering down the road about six months ago."

The woman's expression never changed.

"Anyway," Joe continued, "our daughter, Lilly, wanted to give you these things that belonged to her brother."

"It's just some books and clothes and toys," Lilly added, and then asked, "What's the baby's name?"

"His name's Joshua." She didn't bother to blow her cigarette smoke away from our faces. "You can leave that shit there on the porch if you want to." Then she started to close the door.

As the door was closing, I slid my foot between the jamb and the door. I turned toward Joe and said, "Take Lilly and get in the car." I pushed the door open and went inside. The baby's mother backed away from me and she looked a little scared. Maybe she thought I was a cop or a social worker or that I was going to take Joshua away from her. Whoever she thought I was, I could see she hated me, hated her life probably, hated Joshua, and hated the baby she was carrying. But right now, I pretty much hated her too, as much for being pregnant as for how she'd treated Lilly.

"Apparently, my nine-year-old daughter cares more about your son than you do." I walked closer to her and stuck my finger in her face. "She thinks you won't buy Joshua books, so she gathered up ones that she's outgrown and asked us to bring her out here so she could give them to him. And you treat her like she's garbage. The clothes and the books and toys aren't much, but they mean a lot to her for reasons you don't need to know. And you have the nerve to call it shit."

I backed up a little when I realized that I might be scaring Joshua. "You don't deserve him, you know, or that baby you're carrying—smoking around Joshua's bad enough, but you're even too selfish to stop when you're pregnant. Someone ought to report you to Protective Services. And I might be just the someone who does it." And I turned around to leave.

She started to yell as I left, "You fuckin bitch! Get the fuck out of my house. You don't know shit about shit. How'd I know you weren't coming here to steal my son? Maybe, I'll be the one reporting you."

Joe waited outside the door. I wasn't sure how much of it he'd heard?

Joe waited outside the door. "Good for you. Lilly, your mother just gave that lady not only a piece of her mind, but a whole lot of shoe leather to go along with it."

I could feel my eyes tearing up and that burning in my chest that I get when I'm scary angry. I was frightened because I felt like I could have physically hurt the woman.

"What'd you say to her mom?"

"I just told her that she didn't deserve that little boy or any child for that matter." I didn't mention her being pregnant. I wasn't going to say anything about it if they hadn't noticed.

"I'm sorry, honey." Lilly looked disappointed and on the verge of tears.

As we drove toward home, I asked Joe, "What would make a person be so cold and heartless?"

"Maybe somebody she was close to died or left her," Lilly said. "I'm still glad we did it."

"I'm glad we know his name now. What made you think to ask about it?"

Lilly started to cry. "I thought, for sure, she'd say his name was Ben. Then it'd be like he'd replaced our Ben."

"Is that why you wanted to come out here," Joe asked, "to find out his name?"

"That was only part of it. I mostly wanted him to have Ben's things. I like thinking about Joshua, picturing him playing with

Ben's toys and wearing his clothes. I don't really know why."

"It's a way to keep Ben's spirit alive," I said. "Just like when you gave his bike to that other boy. Besides a few special keepsakes, it's probably time we took the rest of his things to Goodwill."

"The little guy had really grown, hadn't he—no thanks to her," I said. "I wonder where that awful man was?"

"I'm glad he wasn't around," Lilly said. We all agreed.

I stayed at the house for supper and worked on some homework with Lilly. "That was a really fine thing you did today." I said. "We can't control the way other people act. We just have to do what we think we're supposed to do and not worry about any kind of reward. What you did was right for you, and for dad and me, and even for Ben. But mostly it was right for Joshua."

Lilly smiled, but I could tell she was still disappointed. Joe and I tucked her into bed before I left to go back to the Sorry Cabin.

Neither of them mentioned the fact that the baby's mother was pregnant.

On the drive back, I couldn't get the image of the baby out of my mind. It was not the image of him today, but from six months ago. Here I hadn't even thought about him for months and suddenly I'm seeing that tiny neglected baby all alone. I tried to figure out why I had gone off on his mother so badly.

That night I dreamt I'd gone away and left a baby alone at home, then remembered him later when we were too far to return to get him. It wasn't a baby I recognized in the dream, just some faceless baby. I wondered what my mind was doing—playing tricks, maybe—replacing one obsession with another. At least I was not seeing Ben fall. Not that this image was much better; but why an abandoned baby? The image of the baby didn't seem like it had anything to do with Ben.

The next morning after breakfast, and after a brief and cold stint in the swing, I decided to open one of those cans of green paint. I had to do something to get rid of the image of that forlorn child. The previous painting I'd done had felt therapeutic. It was physical, yet contemplative, plus it'd left me with a sense of accomplishment. I could see the results right away.

I didn't worry about the temperature, whether or not it was too cold to paint. It was early December and still in the high forties and it would likely get into the fifties later in the day. The sycamore was bare and most of the oak leaves had fallen. But the cedars and hemlocks were almost as green as they'd been in the summer.

Even though it was the same color as Ben's bedroom, it looked different in the outside light. It was the color of a Florida lime—bright green with a hint of lemons. I painted for hours. I stopped only to step back and admire my progress. Images of the baby continued to flash, how he'd reached out his arms and said "Up," when I had grabbed him from the road. Then I saw his mother—pregnant—smoking.

I painted. I ate. I slept. I painted more.

The dry wood absorbed the paint like a sponge. By the end of Tuesday, the second day of painting, there were two coats on two sides of the Sorry Cabin. What a difference it made. When I get finished, we might have to come up with a new name for the place, I thought.

When I called home that night Lilly was filled with excitement. Around 4:30 that afternoon they'd ridden past the baby's house again, at her insistence, and the box was gone from the front porch. Lilly was sure it meant that Joshua's mom had brought the box inside and that he was now playing with all Ben's things.

"Maybe we should get him a cat," Lilly said.

I knew Joe would never let that happen, so I skipped the lecture and asked her about school. We talked for about five more minutes and she handed the phone off to Joe.

"Are you going to let her talk you into a cat for Joshua now?" I kidded. Then imitating Lilly, I said, "If his mom won't let him have it, we could just keep it here, Dad, but it'll still be Joshua's cat."

"Wouldn't surprise me if that isn't exactly what she'd say." Joe laughed.

I told him about the images of the baby and about painting the house.

"You'll have to tell me more about this baby thing. How about Lilly and I come out on Saturday and help you paint.

"Why don't you come Friday night and spend the night. We can build a fire. I'll make spaghetti. Bring George and Marcel too. Clementine could use a good fight."

Joe laughed. "I've got Shamus coming over for an hour or so to be with Lilly after school tomorrow. I'm going for drinks with some of the other teachers. They keep telling me I need to get out more. I thought it might shut them up for a while if I go this once."

"Well, have fun. You certainly deserve a night out."

The next day I painted the trim around the windows. This was a more tedious job and called for considerably closer concentration. I was bent close to the glass when an image of a room with someone on a bed or a table rushed into my memory. The room actually looked like a kitchen, but it was dark and scary. When the image returned, I saw that it was me on the table. At first I thought—well, at least it's not the baby or Ben falling.

I dropped the paintbrush and staggered back a few steps. I rounded the corner of the house and found my way to the swing and sat down. It wasn't as though I'd forgotten, but had stuffed the incident so deep for so long, I could almost deny its ever happening. I closed my eyes and the memory came gushing through.

I was sixteen and hadn't told anyone that I was pregnant. I'd heard about an old woman who had taken care of girls who had "got themselves in trouble." I told my parents I was spending the night with a girlfriend.

I gave the old woman all my birthday and babysitting money, but she gave it back to me, saying "Use this money for something that makes you happy." She told me to sit down at the table. There were three pouches of what looked like herbs wrapped in cheesecloth. She handed me a card with instructions on how to make tea with the herbs. Her writing was formal, almost calligraphic and a little hard to read.

She said, "If you're not too far gone, these ought to work. But if they don't, come back next Saturday and we'll do what we have to do." She patted my hand almost motherly; not judging or condemning in any way.

"Most girls bring somebody with them," she said when I returned the following Saturday. "Boyfriend, girlfriend, mother. Take a swig of this whiskey." It was in a Mason jar. "It'll help relax you."

I said nothing and drank the shot of whiskey. I lay down on the table and covered up with a clean white sheet. The old woman put a black apron on over her long gray dress. If I hadn't known better I might have thought she was a nun. She had long graying hair that was pulled back into a braid. Mostly I remember her eyes, they were as gray as her dress. When I looked at her more closely, she was plainly beautiful.

She used some type of instruments, but I never felt any pain. She talked to me in a quiet voice the whole time. "I know what you're feeling. I was in this same situation when I was a girl." She told me I hadn't done anything sinful, that all of that "right and wrong, good and bad business" was made up by politicians, priests, and preachers.

I was dumbfounded at the clarity of this memory that I'd secreted away for so many years. I was sure the words are not verbatim, but I could hear her in my head like it was yesterday.

She said there would be people who will judge me, but I shouldn't listen to them. Then she said, "Here's the last thing I have to say—if you've told someone about this, that's okay, but don't tell anybody else, because it's not likely they will understand. If you need to talk, you can always come back here."

"We're all finished, now get some sleep, child."

It was daylight when I woke up. She was wearing the same gray dress when she handed me a cup of very strong coffee. "Drink this," she said. "You'll be fine."

She teased about how we both had funny names, but I don't remember hers.

"Yes ma'am," I said, looking directly into those gray eyes. Then I left.

Never telling anyone must have caused me to hide the memory in a very deep place. But, I'd always known it was there somewhere. With senior year and graduation and college approaching, I pushed it out of my consciousness. Since I would have preferred that it had never happened, I guess I chose to think about other things. I remember at checkups after Ben and Lilly were born, whenever I was asked how many pregnancies I'd had, I always said two.

To this day, I'm glad I kept it to myself. My mother would have been so ashamed of me. It was always her worst fear—that my sisters or I might disgrace her in some way.

Now, what do I do? I've lost two children. Maybe I'm not fit to raise Lilly or any child. I was no different than Joshua's mother. Maybe that's what Joe would think if I told him about the abortion.

I sat in the swing in the cold until dark, when I remembered the paint and the dropped brush on the other side of the house. I cleaned up my mess and built a fire in the fireplace. I poured a glass of wine and wondered how a person can choose to forget, the way I had.

I called Lilly around seven o'clock that night.

"Shamus and I ordered a pizza," she said. "Dad left us some money. Shamus helped me with my math homework and now we're watching a *Laverne and Shirley* rerun on Nickelodeon."

"Okay," I said. "I guess I'll see you and dad tomorrow night, then."

The bed was still folded out from the morning, and I fell asleep in my clothes still recalling small pieces of that sixteen-year-old girl.

It was too cold to paint or to sit in the swing on Friday. If Lilly and Joe hadn't been coming out that night, I would probably have spent the day on the couch in front of the fire. But, I had promised them spaghetti.

I hadn't slept well. There were too many memories—the abortion, Joshua and his pregnant mother, Ben. I felt like I was falling back into the same abyss from which I was just beginning to emerge. Not now, I thought, not when I was almost starting to feel better.

It occurred to me that Joe and I had never really talked about abortion as a political issue. We'd spent hours discussing war and the ERA and the death penalty, but never abortion. I wondered why? I thought I knew almost everything about him, but not this. I couldn't predict how he'd respond. Would he shrug it off? Maybe

I'd better not tell him. I'd gone a long time without saying anything, why upset things now?

I chopped onions and garlic for the red sauce. I put it on early to make sure it would be thick and rich and savory, and also, because I liked how it made the cabin smell like a real home. Joe had said that he'd bring fresh bread and real butter. I would wait until just before we served it to grate the Parmesan and Romano cheeses.

After I'd bathed and dressed, I did spend a long part of the day on the couch napping and reading. I'd had a cord of wood delivered in early November so I could have as many fires as I pleased. I kept it blazing the entire day.

When it started getting dark, I lit a few candles. For a Sorry Cabin, it was starting to seem quite cozy and forgiving.

Joe got there before five thirty. When he walked in the door, he was alone. "Is Lilly still in the car?"

He put down the cat carrier and said, "Lilly's spending the night with her friend Marissa, I didn't think you'd mind. It's the first time any of her girlfriends have invited her since . . ." and his voice trailed off. "Marissa's mother's dropping her off here around one or two o'clock tomorrow on her way to Elizabethtown. So you'll still get to see her. I hope you're not disappointed."

"Of course not, I think it's wonderful and normal for her to want to go to her friend's house. I'm glad you let her go." I was so surprised by Lilly's absence that I didn't say anything about how tired Joe seemed. He had dark circles under his eyes and he looked like he'd lost weight.

"She was pretty excited about it."

I had started to set the table, while Joe walked around the cabin examining the curtains and the candles and the fire. "This is not the same old shack. I'm amazed."

"How about a glass of wine?" I asked. "I have red or white."

"With pasta and red sauce, red, of course."

We moved the table in front of the hearth. We ate the spaghetti and soaked up the sauce and olive oil with our bread. By about seven-thirty, we'd finished the entire bottle of red wine. Joe opened another.

We moved the table back to its spot under the window, and sat on the floor with our backs to the couch. We sipped our wine and stared at the fire. We talked about Lilly, and Joe said, "Oh, my parents called and want to come visit us again this May. I said, maybe we'd go up there. It just seems too soon and too hard to see them here again."

"Have you told them that I've been staying here?"

"No, but I haven't tried to hide it either. Lilly might have said something. They don't ask."

I could tell this wasn't a good time to bring up the abortion. "I'm glad you suggested that they not come."

We watched George and Marcel try to attack Clementine. The old girl looked at them with one eye open, and sent them scurrying with her gaping yawn. Joe and I laughed at their antics.

"Let's open the couch out and get under the covers," Joe said. "I'm freezing my ass off. I'll stoke up the fire."

The fire roared as we crawled under the covers. We'd shared a bed after Ben's accident but we hadn't made love until tonight. The foldout had never been so comfortable and warm. Joe was slow and quiet and let me take as much time as I wanted. The way our bodies had always moved together came back to us like it had just been yesterday. Being touched made me aware of my body again.

But it was the kissing, so warm, so intimate and loving—that's what I couldn't give or get enough of—those kinds of kisses that are long and slow when you don't really know which of you is the kisser, that go down to your neck and back to your mouth. That's how we kissed tonight. I hadn't realized how much I'd missed him or his kisses.

With the food and the wine and the lovemaking, we were both asleep by ten o'clock.

I woke up to the smell of coffee and more kisses. "How long have you been up?" I asked. "Is it late?"

"It's ten after eight. You'd better get your sorry ass out of that sorry bed and fix me some breakfast, woman."

"How about left over spaghetti?" I joked.

We rekindled the fire with fresh twigs and logs, and sat around drinking coffee until almost ten. Once we were showered and dressed, I took Joe out to see the paint.

"I am very impressed with your brush skills, lady. Unfortunately, I think it might be too cold to paint today. I don't think you're supposed to paint when it's below thirty degrees."

"I knew you'd figure out a way to wiggle out of helping me."

We went for a hike in the woods. It was cold and dreary and looked like it might snow.

"By the way, what time did you get home Thursday night? When I talked to Lilly, it was around seven and you were still out."

"I came in right when she was hanging up the phone. We got busy talking at the bar, and I lost all track of time. Lilly was fine, she didn't even realize I was late."

"So, you had a good time. I'm glad!"

I thought this might be my only chance to tell him about the abortion, so I said, "Joe, there's something I need to talk about. It's something that happened a long time ago, that I've never told anyone."

"Go ahead." We turned and headed toward the Sorry Cabin.

"Remember, I told you about how those images of Joshua in the road kept popping into my mind and about my dream of leaving a baby all alone? Well, when I was painting the trim on the window on Thursday, another image popped up. It was of a teenage girl lying on a table. She was having an abortion in this old lady's kitchen."

"What was that all about?" Joe asked.

"It was me, Joe. I've never admitted it to anyone, but when I was sixteen I got knocked up by my jerk of a boyfriend and I found out about this old woman who did that sort of thing, and she helped me take care of it."

Joe had stopped walking. I turned around and looked at him. "How could your parents ever let you do such a thing?"

"I never told them. I never told anybody until this very minute."

"That seems pretty weird to me. How do you not tell something for twenty-five years and then suddenly decide to? I mean, wouldn't it have been a pretty significant event? I would think a person might need to talk about having aborted their baby."

"Joe, what's wrong with you? I was only sixteen. It was the only thing I thought I could do. I couldn't disappoint my parents."

"Let's go inside," he said. "It's getting colder."

I made popcorn thinking we could hold off for a late lunch, early supper of leftover pasta with Lilly.

I tried to talk to Joe. "Do you think what I did was wrong?"

"Of course it was wrong. If you didn't want it, you could've given it up for adoption. You didn't have to kill it."

I wanted to argue with him, but instead my heart sank. When would I learn to keep my mouth shut? I was still not completely convinced that it hadn't been my screaming at Ben that caused him to fall off the rail before the tree hit it a second later. Now this! I had not had to tell Joe about the abortion, so why did I do it? I couldn't bear that I had disappointed him so profoundly.

I was shocked by his reaction, although I probably shouldn't have been. I'd just assumed that we agreed on the issue. I had no idea how far apart we were.

Until Marissa's mom dropped Lilly off, Joe and I talked very little. He busied himself with the fire and restocking the hearth logs.

Lilly's arrival livened things up a bit with her retelling every minute of her sleepover. "We watched *Annie*, and then Marissa's dad took us to get ice cream. We stayed up really late playing with her Nintendo. It was really cool." She sat on the floor with George and Marcel and Clementine and almost fell asleep before we could get supper on the table.

I had thought they would spend the night. But as soon as the supper dishes were cleaned up, Joe said, "We better get you home Lil, you look pretty tired."

"I thought you were staying tonight," I said quietly to Joe.

"Lilly will rest better at home. I can't have her too tired for school on Monday."

I turned toward Joe and caught his gaze. His eyes were cold and eerily vacant, and I saw again how tired he looked. It felt as though we'd turned a corner. It just wasn't the one I'd hoped for.

I tried one more time. "Joe, I'm still the same person that I was yesterday, not one thing about me has changed. You're the one who's different."

"I can't talk about this now. I'll call you tomorrow."

I carried Lilly up to the car. Joe followed with their bags and the cats.

As they pulled away, I felt as though the last blanket of security in my life had just been shredded. He was the one person I could always depend on. No matter what happened in our lives, Joe had always been solidly on my side. I would never have survived Ben's death if Joe hadn't been so caring and supportive, and so much more so than I'd been of him. Now, it wasn't just that he wasn't supporting me—he was against me. In just a matter of hours, everything had fallen apart. But then that's the way Joe had always been—taking up for people who couldn't take up for themselves.

Sunday was one of those spectacular late fall, early winter days. It warmed into the forties and the sky was as blue and cloudless as you could ever wish for. I sat in the purple swing and watched red tail hawks soar overhead and squirrels scratch the ground for buried acorns. I wanted to sit there all day, but I would've only felt sorry for myself. So, I painted. I was able to get a coat on the two unpainted sides of the cabin before it started to get dark and too cool.

Even though I thought about all that had gone on yesterday and on Friday, I didn't let it stop me. I refused to let Joe's opinion of me become my own. It was hard enough just to have told him about it. For Joe to judge me so harshly was incomprehensible. He was judging me as I am today, not as that frightened sixteen-year-old. As much as I tried to make sense of it, I couldn't.

Lilly called about seven. She had just finished her homework. I asked her if she had recuperated from Friday night.

"I'm not tired any more; we just sat around all day, anyway. Dad watched stupid football. It was weird," she whispered. "He asked me if I wanted to go to church with him this morning. I said 'No way.'"

"Really?" I said in disbelief. Joe never watched football. He thought it was violent and overly macho. On the other hand, he loved baseball. He'd always tried to get Ben to understand the philosophical side of baseball—how there were no time constraints and you scored points by running in a circle toward home. I don't think Ben ever quite understood. I know I didn't. But, this thing about Joe considering going to church; that made me very nervous.

"I'm not sure Dad's okay," she said. "Maybe you should come home."

"I'm sure Dad's fine." I said. "You don't need to worry."

Again, I made a decision. It was not a decision based on reason. It was a decision based on need. Joe and Lilly needed me.

I hardly slept that night thinking about Joe. The next evening I called him. Lilly answered as usual, and handed the phone off to her dad. His "hello" sounded a little distant and cool but not as angry as before.

"I think it's time for me to move back home. I feel better now—so much stronger than before, and I've almost finished painting the cabin. What if I move home this weekend?"

"I'll borrow the truck again," he said. "Lilly and I'll be out Saturday morning."

It had occurred to me overnight that it might not be as much about the abortion Joe was reacting to as it was his grief. Maybe the anger and disappointment he felt was more about his sorrow or his inability to grieve for Ben. I left so soon after Ben died that he'd hardly had time to think. He had to take care of me and of Lilly and everything else—all by himself. My telling him about the abortion had likely given him the excuse he needed to grieve over a helpless child, to get angry at the unfairness, the irrationality of it all—just how I'd felt after Ben died.

Joe and I didn't talk the rest of the week. Either Lilly called or she answered the phone when I called. I didn't ask to talk to him. I figured he needed the time.

I put the second coat of paint on the cabin and finished the trim. When it was complete, I stepped back to admire what I'd accomplished during the last five months. The run-down shack had been turned into a cheerful and whimsical cottage. I could picture flower boxes bursting with dahlias and impatiens under the windows in the spring and summer, and a fresh pine wreath on the door in winter. The little house looked like it could have been sitting in the midst of the Black Forest or in the Irish countryside. Even Ben might have thought it pretty, though he would likely have complained about the purple.

THE WOODS: A REFLECTION

The kitchen is silent save the *tick, tick, tick* of four boiling brown eggs pecking at the aluminum pan on the stove. It's the only pot I've left unpacked. I watch out the window at the woods and go over and over the list of chores to finish by morning. An evening mist hovers over tufts of verdant moss. The movers arrive tomorrow by nine. I vacillate between exhilaration and despair over the prospects of leaving this place—our home for forty years—though ragged might best describe my mood as it cloaks my boney arms and shoulders like a well-worn, once-lavender shawl. With one last night to reminisce and engrave each corner and cackle into clips of recollection, I wish Joe could be here too, but his recuperation from a stroke is taking longer than expected.

He'd make this night fun or at least funny.

I've carefully chosen my clothes for moving day. A day you wouldn't typically think of dressing for except in something old and worn out; something you wouldn't mind getting dirty or ripped. Instead, I've chosen the gray skirt and tunic I wore to our son Ben's funeral twenty-eight years ago. Moving feels funereal to me as it is an occasion of passing, a departure; but, there is something celebratory about it too—if not of a life in particular, the living of four lives—our lives—mine, Joe's, Lilly's, and Ben's. But further even than leaving the house, the home, the edifice, tomorrow I will say good-bye to the trees, this beloved woods.

It's this woods that chaperone the house that might have caused us to move away, and yet, it's this very woods that has kept us from leaving—the place and each other.

After our son, Ben, died when an ash tree fell on the deck where he was sitting, I needed to blame someone, so on top of blaming myself, I blamed the tree. I blamed the tree even though it and its kind had always been my greatest source of inspiration and insight, starting when I was a girl in Gray Hampton and continuing in the woods here behind our home in Louisville, and even at the Sorry Cabin, a remote shack of sorts where I went to heal after Ben died. I have always sought counsel from the maples, oaks, and even the spindly sassafras trees that populate the woods, and that continue to inhabit these grounds.

The tree that fell had appeared in perfect health, when in fact, it was rotten on the inside. It had even leafed out beautifully that year. Then, like the proverbial "last straw" dropped as delicately as a tear upon the back of a camel, the decayed wood could bear no more and the ash tree gave way to the weight of its leaves and its limbs and that scintilla of new growth it had sprouted overnight.

Call it coincidence or serendipity that we happened to be there, that Ben was in the path of the tree's falling arc just at the perfect moment in time. It had been a providential point in our lives for many reasons, but this? It couldn't have happened more flawlessly if we'd planned it.

At seventy, I now see that blaming the tree was as ridiculous as blaming the clock for the passage of time. Though it does appear that the movement of the hands on the dial and the turning of the pages of the calendar have progressed in direct correlation with the sagging of my skin and my memory. Still, just as the tree is not an executioner, the timekeepers are not the conspirators of my aging.

I have implored the woods and every tree that has sprung up since that awful day to forgive my betrayal. It is possible, if not probable, that we were actually the cause of the tree's decay to begin with—by digging deck footings too close to its roots and causing the ground around it to erode. Chalk it up to humanity, as only humans would need something or someone to blame. Chalk it up to humanity to think that absolution is a prerequisite to the washing away of guilt.

With so much to ask forgiveness for—having determined myself to be a less than ideal daughter, a less than dutiful wife, and never the doting mother—it makes no sense that now I feel nothing that can not be construed as appreciation. I can see how others might find this sense of gratitude counterintuitive, inhumane maybe, given that I have lost a child, almost lost a marriage, and came close to alienating my daughter; but I have come to realize that most things just do not make sense.

After Ben died, I knew I was leaving my husband and daughter to fend for themselves when I holed up in a cabin for five months, thinking I could figure it all out—by thinking. Like the trees, Joe and Lilly never felt a need to blame or forgive me even though I considered my leaving an egregiously selfish act. But I had learned the benefits of quiet and solitude from my stepfather, Louis, in Gray Hampton, where I grew up, and I knew I needed silence in order to grieve and to heal; to see who I was when not in relation to another. As Melville said, "Silence is the only voice of God," and silence is what I needed to hear.

For five months, I sat in a porch swing and breathed and silently listened and paid close attention to the trees; and I painted (not the artistic kind of painting, but the house-coating type).

And I swung. Swinging was another solitary pastime I had learned in Gray Hampton while swaying on my grandmother Mam's front porch and then in the one we'd hung in the woods here.

When it came time to leave the cabin, I had come to simply accept the facts. There was no figuring it out—a tragedy had happened and it had happened to me and to my family; just as it happens to many families without "rhyme nor reason" as Shakespeare so fittingly put it. So, how could I think it should not happen to me?

My own mother, a woman already embittered as a result of the circumstances of her youth, lost her husband when she was a young woman. She had two girls and was pregnant with a third when he died. She did not have the option of going off to breathe, or swing, or to pay heed to the trees; she had to find work to support her family. She could not afford such self-indulgence. Sal Skinner Barkley Craycroft would have called me irresponsible, and given the standards and "values" of her era, she'd have been right. But, back then the world was busy learning ways to harness and control nature, and most folks had no concern with finding their place in it.

Sal found no comfort in trees. Her wounded heart even knotted the ones in our yard into a nuisance. She constantly feared their falling on our house (an anxiety that now, ironically, seems all the more foreboding); she saw the acorns that dropped in the fall as untidy, and the squirrels they attracted as vermin, and the expansive leafy canopy prevented any grass from growing into a respectable lawn. I'm sure if she'd had the funds or a sturdy saw, she would have felled the gentle giants posthaste. Lucky for the trees and me she was not a wealthy woman.

Sal's passing began around Christmas when she was only sixty-seven years old. There were subtle signs. She was quieter, and too young to be staggering and so unsteady on her feet. Then, in March there was a stumble on level ground at a shopping center that resulted in a broken hip, a hospital stay, a hip replacement, a CAT scan, and the discovery of several dime-sized inoperable tumors located deep in her brain.

The next June, my oldest sister, Nicole, and her entire family moved from another state to assume the task of taking care of Sal in her last days. Nicole cared for her lovingly and faithfully—even though some might have said that it was more than Sal deserved. Still, we loved her for some reason—not just because she had mellowed in those later years, nor just because she loved her grandchildren with a passion that seemed to have skipped a generation. I assume it was just because she needed for us to love her. She died quietly at home that following September with her arm reaching toward something only she could name.

It is said that the acorn falls not far from the tree, and our daughter Lilly now lives in the Sorry Cabin in Gray Hampton, with her partner Julien and his two children Milo and Larken. It's situated in the outskirts of the town I grew up in. "Sorry" is what we called the old cabin I stayed in for those five months after Ben died. It has been in the family for generations. Lilly and Julien have turned the old shack into quite a showplace, but everyone still calls it the Sorry Cabin. Lilly has pleaded with Joe and me to move there, but we still enjoy our independence and the benefits of living in the city—the people, the doctors, the houses, the movies, the shopping, the restaurants—we have a long list of reasons.

What's even better is that Lilly works in a research forest. Over the years, she has treated Joe and me to sections of the forest that the public doesn't normally get to see. We've spent many an evening there on our backs, listening to the squeaks of the peeps in the lake luring their mates, watching the night sky slowly brighten into a Joan Mitchell canvas, and stumbling upon the ephemeral formations of rocks, leaves or sticks constructed by guerilla artists, both human and non.

But there is something to be said for having your own personal woods like ours, where you know each tree by the furrows and ridges of its bark and by the scent of its roots, and where those same trees know Joe and me just as well. When walking beneath the sylvan baldachin, my whole being blends with the essence of the timber and the flora and just for a second, I know who I am. It is no longer merely woods, it is a community of trees, a coterie of wisdom—only without their ever intending to be such, without ever intending anything but being trees.

Well, as predictably as leaves falling in autumn, the season has arrived for Joe and me to depart from this ordinary house and these extraordinary woods and these unremarkable memories. There are trees surrounding the yellow house where we're moving, but they're mostly newly planted. And I can always drive to the forest for a few hours to get my woods fix, as there are nurses to watch after Joe when I can't be here. A stroke has left him with some paralysis on his left side, but Dr. Lane says, in time, he'll be as good as new. As soon as he can get out, we'll head for the trees.

Being without Joe these weeks and being seventy, my days and nights can get particularly reminiscent. Lately, I have thought about an old woman from my youth who helped me out of a potentially life-altering situation. Like I said, I had not been an ideal daughter and when I was sixteen I became pregnant. I sought the old woman out having heard about her from other girls who'd heard about her from older girls. Unlike the butchers you read about and the coat hanger procedures with their resulting infections and sterility, she was a skilled medicine woman. When I remember that time, I can still feel the overwhelming desperation and shame gripping my gut that she helped quash. She was that rare person who had realized her calling (despite its illegality) and she carried it out with the elegance of a priestess—judging, it seemed, neither her own deeds nor mine. Maybe I learned something from this kindly abortionist about disapproving and condemning. I had expected deprecation and aspersion from her for my scandalous behavior, but I received only support and caring, so contrary to what I had expected from her and from everyone else—had I told them.

Might Sal have contemplated a similar course of action once the irreversible and transcendent results of her widowhood began to soak in? I've asked myself this question a hundred times. Who would have blamed her for such a consideration? Raising two children on your own is burdensome enough, without adding a third child to the mix where problems become geometrically compounded—triangulated. Once again, lucky for me she didn't choose abortion, and not so fortunate for my own jettisoned embryo.

So strong is this desire to understand things from the past that all too often I try to live life backwards just to try to make it all make sense; but that is only human folklore and myth. I think about the past even though I know there's nothing to be gained by looking there. Still, Joe and I talk and laugh and even occasionally weep about silly and not-so-silly times and events in our marriage. It is, after all, only human to reflect; to ponder, muse, ruminate and second-guess decisions and choices and judgments.

Chalk it up to humans to resist our inner nature. Chalk it up to the trees and to nature to never question, to never ask "why," to simply accept what life sends their way without needing an answer or an explanation . . . breathing and listening.

I crack and peel one brown egg, then another, revealing the white, heat-hardened albumen under their thin shells. I know I should eat, but eating another meal alone, if only two boiled eggs, is hardly worth the effort.

When the cellphone rings, I know it's Joe. He's checking on me and on my packing progress.

"Have you eaten?" he asks.

"I just boiled some eggs," I answer, dashing salt and pepper on the skins. With my mouth full, I ask him, "How was PT today?"

"Just another round of *pain and torture.*" I groan at the worn-out joke, knowing neither the joke nor the PT is actually funny.

"Have you packed the art?" Joe wants to know. It's a long-running joke between us. I call the stuff on the walls *pictures*, Joe calls it *art.* In truth, it's a combination—a few pieces that could be considered *art*, the rest are prints and photos.

"I'm saving that for the movers, I wouldn't want the *art* to get damaged from my flimsy wrapping."

"Say *bye* to the house and the woods for me," he says.

"Say it yourself, I'll hold the phone out the window."

"You're impossible," he says with a laugh, slightly slurring the *s*.

ACKNOWLEDGMENTS

I am grateful to my family, those around me now as well as the ones who have passed on. Special thanks go to George, Drew, Kate, Stella, Theo, and Phyllis. To the trees in Cherokee Park, Bernheim Forest, the Loretto Motherhouse, and especially to the ordinary silver maple in my side yard, I pay homage for your inspiration and guidance.

Thanks also to the much loved literary treasures—Silas House, Robin Lippincott, "Elner" Morse, and Sena Jeter Naslund for your close reading and sage counsel. To Nana Lampton for the use of your writing cottage at Tirbracken, I am eternally appreciative. Other friends and colleagues whose support and generosity have been invaluable include Dianne Aprile, Kathleen Driskell, Weezie Gulick, Rachel Harper, the Kraub Farmers, Connie Kuhn, Ellyn Lichvar, Monica Mahoney, Karen Mann, Ali Matthews, Phil Samuel, Katy Yocom, and Sam Zalutsky. And lastly, thanks to Bob Hill for saying to me, "you are a writer."

ABOUT THE AUTHOR

Gray Hampton is Gayle Hanratty's first book. Her short stories have appeared in *Monkscript*, *The Louisville Review*, and *Trajectory*, where she was co-winner of their inaugural short story contest. Gayle lives in Louisville with her husband George. She is a graduate and retired staff member of Spalding University's Masters of Fine Arts in Writing Program. In addition to writing, she creates terrariums in tribute to the forest floor.

Fleur-de-Lis Press is named to celebrate the life

of Flora Lee Sims Jeter

(1901–1990)